THE BOBBSEY TWINS AT SNOW LODGE

The welcome light shone out through the storm and darkness.

THE BOBBSEY TWINS AT SNOW LODGE

by LAURA LEE HOPE

Book-of-the-Month Club
New York

The Bobbsey Twins at Snow Lodge was first published in 1913.

ISBN: 1-58288-135-9

Printed in the United States of America

CONTENTS

CONTENTS

CHAPTER 1

THE RUNAWAYS

"WILL Snap pull us, do you think, Freddie?" asked little Flossie Bobbsey as she anxiously looked at her small brother, who was fastening a big shaggy dog to his sled by means of a homemade harness. "Do you think he'll give us a good ride?"

"Sure he will, Flossie," answered Freddie with an air of wisdom. "I explained it all to him, and I've tried him a little bit. He pulled fine, and you won't be much heavier. I'll have the harness all fixed in a minute, and then we'll have a grand ride."

"Do you think Snap will be strong enough to pull both of us?" asked the little girl.

"Of course he will!" exclaimed Freddie firmly. "He's as good as an Eskimo dog, and we saw some pictures of them pulling sleds bigger than ours."

"That's so," admitted Flossie. "Well, hurry up, please, Freddie, 'cause I'm cold standing here, and I want to get under the blankets on the sled and have a nice ride."

"I'll hurry all right, Flossie. You go up there by Snap's head and pat him. Then he'll stand stiller, and I can fix the harness on him quicker."

Flossie, with a shake of her light curls, and a stamp of her little feet to rid them of the snow from the drift in which she had been standing, went closer to the fine-looking and intelligent dog, who did not seem to mind being tied up with ropes and leather straps to Freddie's sled.

"Good old Snap!" exclaimed Flossie, patting his head. "You're going to give Freddie and me a fine ride, aren't you, old fellow?"

Snap barked and wagged his tail violently.

"Hey! Stop that!" cried Freddie. "He's flopping his tail right in my face!" the little boy added. "I can't see to fasten this strap. Hold his tail, Flossie."

Snap, hearing the voice of his young master—one of his two masters by the way—wagged his tail harder than ever. Freddie made a grab for it, but missed. Flossie, seeing this, laughed and Snap, thinking it was a great joke, leaped about and barked with delight. He sprang out of the harness, which was only partly fastened on, and began leaping about in the snow. Finally he stood up on his hind legs and marched about, for Snap was a trick dog and had once belonged to a circus.

"There now! Look at that!" cried Freddie. "He's

spoiled everything! We'll never get him hitched up now."

"It–it wasn't my fault," said Flossie, a tear or two coming into her eyes.

"I know it wasn't, Flossie," replied Freddie, speaking more quietly. "It's always just that way with Snap when he gets excited. Come here!" he called to the dog, "and let me harness you. Come here, Snap!"

The dog was well-enough trained so that he knew when the time for fun was over and when he had to settle down. Still wagging his tail joyously, however, Snap came up to Freddie, who started over again the work of harnessing the animal to the sled.

"I guess you'd better stand at his tail instead of at his head," said Freddie. "So when he wags it you can grab it, Flossie, and hold it still. Then it won't slap me in the face, and I can see what I'm doing. Hold his tail, Flossie."

"Then he can't wag it," objected the little girl.

"I know he can't. I don't want him to."

"But it may make him angry."

"Snap never gets mad, do you, Snap?" asked Freddie, and the dog's bark seemed to say, "No, never!"

So Flossie held the dog's tail, while Freddie put

on the harness again. This time he succeeded in getting it all arranged to suit him, and the frisky Snap was soon made fast to the sled.

"Now get on, Flossie," called her brother, "and we'll see how fast Snap can pull us."

"But don't make him go too fast, Freddie," begged the little girl. "For it's hard pulling in the snow."

"No, I'll let him go slow," promised Freddie. "But it won't be hard work pulling us. My sled goes awfully easy, anyhow."

Freddie tucked Flossie in amid the robes and rugs that the children had taken from the house, near where they had started to harness the dog. Then Freddie took his place in front of his sister, holding on to two reins that were fastened to the dog's head. Freddie had made no bit, such as is used for horses and goats, but he thought by making straps fast to a sort of muzzle he could guide Snap, by pulling his head to one side or the other.

"All ready, Flossie?" called Freddie, when he himself was comfortable on the sled.

"All ready," she answered.

"Giddap, Snap!" cried Freddie, and, with a bark, off the dog started, pulling the sled and the two children after him.

"Oh, he's going! He's giving us a ride! It's as real

as anything!" cried Flossie in delight, holding fast to the sled. "Oh, Freddie!"

"Of course it's real!" said Freddie. "Bert and Nan said Snap wouldn't pull us, but I knew he would. I just wish they could see us now."

As if in answer to this wish a little later, when the two smaller twins had turned a corner, they saw coming toward them their brother and sister Nan and Bert, also twins, but four years older.

"Look, look!" cried Flossie to Nan. "See what a nice ride we're having."

"Oh, look, Bert!" exclaimed Nan. "Snap really is pulling them," and she grasped her brother's arm. Bert was pulling his own sled and that of his twin sister.

"Yes, he'll pull them a little way," admitted Bert, as if he knew all about it, "and then, the first thing they know, Snap will turn around short and tip them into a snowdrift. He hasn't been trained to pull a sled, no matter how many other tricks he can do."

"I trained him myself!" declared Freddie, as he pulled on the lines to bring the dog to a stop. But Snap, seeing Nan and Bert, was eager to reach them to be patted and made much of, so he did not obey the command given by the reins, but kept on.

"Whoa there!" cried Freddie, holding back with all his little strength.

"See, I told you he wouldn't mind," said Bert, with a laugh.

"Oh, but isn't it cute!" exclaimed Nan, clapping her hands. "I didn't think they'd get any ride at all."

"We'll show you! We'll have a fine ride!" panted Freddie, vainly trying to make Snap halt.

Then just what Bert said would happen seemed about to take place. The dog leaped around, and turned short to get nearer to the older Bobbsey twins.

"Look out!" cried Bert, but his warning came too late.

Over went the sled, and Flossie and Freddie were pitched from it into a big, fluffy bank of snow, falling into it deeply, but with no more harm to them than if they had landed on a bed of feathers.

"Oh dear!" cried Flossie, as she felt herself shooting toward the snow.

"Whoa there! Whoa! Don't you run away, Snap!" shouted Freddie. Then his mouth was filled with snow and he could say nothing more.

"Oh, Bert! They'll be smothered!" cried Nan. "Help me get them out!"

Bert was laughing, and trying to defend himself against the jumping up of Snap, who seemed to want to hug the boy with his paws.

"Stop laughing! Help me!" ordered Nan, who

was already trying to lift Flossie from her snowy bed.

"I can't help laughing—Freddie looked so funny when he went over," said Bert. "There's no danger of smothering, though. That snow is as dry as sand. Here you go, Freddie. Give me your hand and I'll pull you out."

In a few seconds the smaller Bobbsey twins stood beside their larger brother and sister, while Snap capered about them, barking loudly and wagging his tail.

"Oh, he's got loose, and the harness is all broken," said Freddie, and tears of disappointment stood in his blue eyes.

"Never mind," said Bert. "I'll help you make a better harness tomorrow, Freddie. That one wasn't strong enough for Snap, anyhow. I'll fix it differently."

"Oh, but we were going to have such a fine ride!" said Flossie, who was also ready to cry. The smaller twins were only about five years old, so it might have been expected.

"Well, come on and go coasting with Bert and me," said Nan, as she patted her little sister's head. "We're going over on the long hill. It's fine there, and you'll have just as much fun as if you had Snap to pull you."

"Shall we go, Freddie?" asked Flossie, who generally depended on him to start their amusements.

"I guess so," he answered. "This harness is all busted, anyhow."

Sadly he looked at the tangled strings and straps fast to the sled, where Snap had broken away from them. The harness Freddie had made with such care was all broken now.

"Never mind," said Bert again. "I'll make you a better one tomorrow, Freddie. Come along now, and we'll have some fun. And when we get through coasting I'll buy everybody a hot chocolate soda."

"Really?" asked Flossie, her sorrow forgotten now.

"Sure thing," promised Bert.

"Come on, then, Freddie," said his little sister. "We can harness Snap up tomorrow."

The useless harness was taken to the Bobbsey home, not far away, and then the four twins—the two sets of them, as it were—started for the coasting hill, Flossie and Freddie having one sled between them, and Nan and Bert each having one of their own.

On the way to the hill they met many of their friends, also bound for the same place. School was just out and the boys and girls were eager to have a good time in the snow.

"There's Charley Mason!" exclaimed Bert, seeing a boy he knew. "Hello, Charley!" he called. "Going coasting?"

"Sure. Where's the big bob?" For some time

before this Bert and Charley had made, in partnership, a large bobsled.

"Oh, I didn't know you'd be out, or I'd have brought it," replied Bert. "Anyhow, I promised Nan I'd coast with her."

"Oh, that's all right. I guess the hill will be too crowded for a bob, anyhow. Danny Rugg was taking his over, though, for I saw him and some of his crowd hauling it from his barn a little while ago."

"Well, let 'em. We can get ours later. Got a new sled?" and Bert looked admiringly at the one Charley was pulling.

"No, it's only my old one painted over. But it makes it look like new."

"We had Snap hitched up, but he broke loose," said Freddie. "But we're going to have a stronger harness tomorrow."

"That's good," said Charley, with a broad smile.

Soon the children were on the hill. There was a large crowd of coasters there, and fun was at its height. There was merry shouting and laughter, and several spills and upsets. As Bert had said, the hill was very much crowded.

"I thought it would be no good for a bob," he remarked.

"There goes Danny Rugg now!" exclaimed Charley. "He's giving orders to everyone."

"He'd better not give any to me," said Bert, in a

quiet voice, but with determination in his tones.

"Oh, Bert!" exclaimed Nan. "Please don't have any fuss, will you?"

"Not on my part," said Bert. "But if Danny Rugg thinks he can boss me he is mistaken."

It was evident that Danny liked to play master. He could be heard giving orders to this one and the other one to get out of the way, to pull his bob around in place, and then to shove it off with its load of boys and girls.

Now, though Danny was a bully, some of the children were friendly with him for the sake of getting a ride on his sled, which was a large and expensive one.

Bert and Nan, and Flossie and Freddie, soon were coasting with their friends, having a good time on the hill. The two smaller twins went down together.

As Freddie came up the long slope, pulling his sled in readiness for another trip, Danny Rugg and his bob reached the head of the slope at the same time.

"Say, Danny, give me a ride this trip, won't you?" begged a small boy, who had no sled but often did errands for the bully and played mean tricks for him that Danny was too lazy to play himself. "Let me go on your bob?"

"Not this time, Sim," said Danny. "The bob is

going to be filled. But here, you can take Freddie Bobbsey's sled. He doesn't want it," and without giving Freddie time to say whether he did or not Danny snatched the sled rope from him and held it out to Sim Watson.

For a moment Freddie was too surprised to utter a protest and then, as he realized what had happened, he cried out, "Here, Danny Rugg, you let my sled alone! I do want it! Give it back to me!"

"Aw, go on!" said Danny. "You've had enough rides. Let Sim take your sled, or I'll punch you!" and Danny gave Freddie a shove, and held out the rope of the sled to Sim.

"Stop it!" cried Freddie. "I'll tell Bert on you."

"Pooh! Think I'm afraid of your brother? I can handle him with one hand tied behind my back."

"Then it's time you started in!" exclaimed a voice just back of Danny, and the bully turned suddenly to see Bert standing near him. Danny's face flushed, and then grew pale. Before he could make a move Bert grabbed away from him the rope of Freddie's sled, which Sim had not yet taken, and passed it back to his small brother.

"Don't you try that again," warned Bert.

"I will if I want to," said Danny, meanly. "I'm not afraid of you."

"Maybe not," said Bert, quietly, "and I'm not afraid of you, either. But if you take my brother's sled for some of your friends you'll have to settle with me. You leave Freddie alone, do you hear?"

"I don't have to mind you!"

"We'll see about that. Go ahead, Freddie. You and Flossie coast as much as you like, and if Danny bothers you anymore let me know."

Danny, with an uneasy laugh, turned aside. Some of his particular chums gathered about him, and one murmured, "Why don't you fight him?"

For a moment it looked as though there might be trouble, but an instant later all thoughts of it passed, for a series of girls' screams came from midway down the long hill.

All eyes were turned in that direction, and those at the top of the slope saw a team of runaway horses, attached to a heavy bobsled plunging madly up the hill.

And, right in the path of the frightened animals was Nan Bobbsey and one or two other girls, on their sleds, coasting straight for the runaways.

A cry of fear came from Bert Bobbsey as he noticed his sister's danger.

CHAPTER 2

OLD MR. CARFORD

"STOP the horses!"

"Yes, grab them, somebody, or they'll run into the girls!"

"Look out, everybody, they're coming right this way!"

"I'm going to get my bob to a safe place!"

It was Danny Rugg who called out this last, and the other boys had shouted the previous expressions, as they watched the oncoming, runaway horses.

Bert Bobbsey had thrown himself on his sled and was coasting toward the group of girls, of whom his sister Nan was one. They were on their sleds in the very path of the team. It seemed that nothing could save them. But Bert had a plan in his mind.

And, while he was preparing to carry it out, I will take just a moment to tell my new readers something about the characters of this story, and the books that have gone before in the series.

Bert and Nan, and Freddie and Flossie Bobbsey were the twin children of Mr. and Mrs. Richard Bobbsey, who lived in an Eastern city called Lakeport, at the head of Lake Metoka. Mr. Bobbsey was a prosperous lumber merchant. Other members of the household were Dinah and Sam Johnson. Dinah was the cook, fat and good-natured. Sam was her husband, slim and also good-natured. He did all sorts of work about the place, from making gardens to shoveling snow.

Then there was Downy, a pet duck; Snoop, a pet black cat; and, of late, Snap, the fine trick dog, who had come into the possession of the Bobbseys in a peculiar manner.

In the first book of this series, entitled *The Bobbsey Twins*, I told of the good times the four children had in their home. How they played in the snow, went coasting, helped to discover what they thought was a "ghost," and did many other things. Bert even went for a sail in an ice boat he and Charley Mason had made, though it was almost more than the boys could manage at times.

The second volume, called *The Bobbsey Twins in the Country*, told of the good times the four had when they went to the farm of Uncle Daniel Bobbsey and his wife, Aunt Sarah, who lived at Meadow Brook.

Such fun as there was!

There was a country picnic, sport in the woods, and a great Fourth of July celebration. A circus gave a chance to have other good times, and though once there was a midnight scare, it all turned out happily.

But though the twins had much happiness in the country they were destined to have still more fun when they went to the ocean shore, and in the third book, called *The Bobbsey Twins at the Seashore*, I related all that happened to them there.

They went on a visit to their uncle, William Minturn, who lived at Ocean Cliff, and their cousin Dorothy showed them many strange scenes and sights. They had most delightful times, and toward the close of their visit there was a great storm at sea, and a shipwreck. The lifesavers were on hand, however, and did such good work that no one was drowned. And if you want to learn how a certain little girl was made very happy when she found that her father was among those saved, you must read the book.

Then, after the storm ceased, there were more happy days at the shore. The time for the Bobbseys to leave came all too soon. School was about to open, and even the smaller twins must now settle down to regular lessons.

In the fourth book of the series, called *The*

Bobbsey Twins at School, there is told of the start for home.

But many things happened before the family arrived. There was the wreck of the circus train, the escape of the animals, the meeting with the very fat lady, and the loss of Snoop, the pet cat. Then, too, a valuable cup the smaller Bobbsey twins had been drinking from, seemed to be lost, and they were very sorry about it.

On the way home something else occurred. They were followed in the dark by some strange animal. At first they feared it was some wild beast from the circus but it proved to be only a friendly dog.

How Flossie and Freddie insisted on keeping the dog, now that their pet cat Snoop was gone, how they named him Snap, and how it was discovered that he could do tricks, are all part of the story.

There were many more happenings after the twins started in at school. Mr. Bobbsey's boathouse caught fire in a mysterious manner. Snap was found to be a circus dog, and it was pretty certain that the fat lady in the train had also belonged to the show, and that it was she who had the valuable silver cup.

In time all was straightened out, and how Snoop came back from the circus in far-off Cuba, how Snap was allowed to stay with the Bobbseys, and how even the cup was finally recovered—all this you will find set down in the fourth book of this series.

And now winter had come in earnest, though even before this story opens the Bobbsey twins had had a taste of snow and ice. The accident on the coasting hill now occupied the attention of all.

"Oh, Nan! Nan will be killed!" cried Flossie, as she stood with Freddie gazing down the slope.

"No, she won't!" exclaimed Freddie. "Bert is going to save her—you'll see!"

"Oh, if he only can!" murmured Nellie Parks, one of Nan's friends.

"I think he will! See, he is coming nearer to them," added Grace Lavine, another friend.

Danny Rugg, mean as he was, was not quite so mean as to discourage this hope. Some of the girls on the sleds that were coming nearer to the rushing horses seemed about to roll off, rather than take chances of steering out of the way of the steeds.

"What can Bert be planning to do?" asked Grace. "How can he save them?"

"I don't know," answered Nellie. "Let's watch him. Maybe he's going to stop the horses."

"He'd never dare!" murmured Grace.

"Oh, Bert is brave," was the answer.

But Bert had no intention of leaping for the horses' heads just now. His first idea was to get his sister and the other girls to a place of safety. As he came near to them, his sled going much faster than theirs, he called out, "Steer to the right! Go to the right! I'll see if I can't make the horses go over to one side."

"All right!" cried Nan, who understood what her brother meant. "Keep to the right, girls," she called to her frightened chums, "and don't any of you fall off!"

Those who had been about to roll from their sleds now held on with firmer clasps. They were close to the runaway team now. Bert was near to them also, and, while wondering to whom they belonged, and whether they had injured their driver or anyone else in their mad rush, he caught up a handful of snow as his sled glided onward.

It was hard work to throw the snowball at the horses, going downhill as he was, but Bert managed to do it. He had the good luck to hit one of the animals with the wad of snow, and this sent the horse over to one side, its mate following. This was just what Bert wanted, as it gave Nan and the others more room to coast past them.

And this is just what the girls did. Their sleds whizzed past the runaways, one sled, on which Hattie Jenson rode, almost grazing a hoof.

"Now you're safe!" cried Bert. "Keep on to the foot of the hill! You're all right!"

He gathered up another handful of snow, and threw it at the steeds, making them swerve more than ever toward the side of the hill. Then one of the animals slipped and stumbled. This caused them both to slow up, and Bert, seeing this, left his sled, rolling off, and letting it go down without him.

Hardly thinking of what he was doing, he ran for the heads of the horses. Perhaps it was not just wise, for Bert was not very tall, but he was brave. However, he was not to stop the runaways all alone, for just then some of the larger boys, who had been rushing down the hill, came up, and before the horses could start off again several lads had grasped them by the bridles and were quieting them.

"That was a good idea of yours, Bert Bobbsey," said Frank Miller. "A fine idea, to throw snowballs at them. It made them go to one side all right, and slowed them up."

"I wanted to save the girls," said Bert, who was panting from his little run.

"Whose team is it?" asked another boy.

"I don't know," answered Bert. "I can't say that I ever saw them before. There's no one in the sled, anyhow, though it is pretty well loaded with stuff."

He and the other boys looked into the vehicle. It contained a number of boxes and bags. Then the boys looked down the hill and saw that the girls who had been in danger were now safe. Nan and the others were walking up, dragging their sleds.

The boys then noticed a man half running up the slope. He was waving his arms in an excited fashion.

"I guess that's the man who owns the horses," said Charley Mason.

There was no doubt of it a few minutes later, when the man came close enough to make himself heard.

"Are they all right, boys?" he asked. "Are my horses hurt?"

"They don't seem to be," answered Frank.

"That's good. Are my things all right?"

"Everything seems to be here," said Charley Mason, who was standing beside Bert. "I know who he is now," went on Charley in a low tone to his chum. "He's Mr. James Carford of Newton."

"He's lame," observed Bert, for the man limped slightly.

"Yes, he was in the war," went on Charley. "He's real rich, too, but peculiar, they say."

By this time aged Mr. Carford was looking over the team and the sled and its contents. He seemed weary and out of breath.

"Yes, everything is all right," he said slowly. "I hope no one was hurt by my runaways. I never knew 'em to do that before. I left 'em outside the store a minute while I went in to get something, and they must have taken fright. I hope no one was hurt."

"No, everyone got out of the way in time," said Bert.

"That's good. Who stopped the horses?" the old man asked.

"Bert Bobbsey," answered Frank Miller. "He warned his sister and the other girls to steer to one side, and then he threw snow at the horses and made them fall down. Then they slowed up so we could grab 'em."

"Ha! Bert Bobbsey did that, eh?" exclaimed aged Mr. Carford. "So this is the second time a Bobbsey has mixed up in my family affairs. The second time," and Mr. Carford looked at Bert in a peculiar manner.

"Did you fall out of the sled, Mr. Carford?" asked another boy, coming up just then.

"No, they started off when I was in the store. Funny, too, that they should. Well, I'm glad there's no one hurt and no damage done. I couldn't walk home to Newton. I'm much obliged to you boys. And to you too, Bert Bobbsey.

"Are you Richard Bobbsey's son?" he suddenly asked, peering at Bert from beneath his shaggy eyebrows.

"Yes, sir."

"Ha! I thought so. You look like him. You do things like him, too, without stopping to be asked. Yes, this is the second time a Bobbsey has meddled with my family affairs. Trying to do me a good turn, I suppose. Well, well!" and he seemed lost in thought.

"What is it? What is the matter?" asked Nan, in a low voice of her brother, as she came to stand beside him. "Is he finding fault because you helped stop his runaway horses?"

"No, Nan. I don't exactly understand what he does mean," answered Bert. "There seems to be some mystery about it."

CHAPTER 3

THE BIG SNOWFALL

FOR a time Mr. Carford seemed more worried about the possible injury to his team, and the loss of some of his goods in the sled, than he was concerned about thanking the boys who had stopped the runaways. Then, as he found by looking over them, that the horses were all right, and that nothing was missing, he approached Bert and the others, saying, "Well, boys, I'm much obliged to you. I can't tell you how much. No telling what damage the horses might have done if you hadn't stopped 'em. And I'm glad no one was hurt.

"Now I reckon you boys aren't much different than I was, when I was a youngster, and I guess you like sweets about the same. Here are a couple of dollars, Bert Bobbsey. I wish you'd treat all your friends to hot chocolate soda or candy or whatever you like best. It isn't exactly payment for what you did, but it just shows I'm not forgetful."

"Oh, we didn't stop the horses for money!"

exclaimed Bert, drawing back.

"I know you didn't," answered Mr. Carford, with a smile, "and I'm not paying you, either. You stopped the horses, or you tried to stop them, Bert, to save your sister and the other girls. I understand that all right. But the horses were stopped just the same, and please take this as a little offering of thanks, if nothing else. Please do."

He held out the two-dollar bill, and Bert did not feel like refusing. He accepted the money with murmured thanks, and as Mr. Carford climbed into the sled, limping more than ever after his run up the hill, the aged man muttered, "The second time a Bobbsey has been mixed up in my affairs. I wonder what will happen when the third time comes?"

Calling good-byes to the boys and girls, and again thanking them for what they had done, Mr. Carford drove off amid a jingle of bells.

"What do you s'pose he meant by saying this was the second time a Bobbsey had been mixed up in his family affairs?" asked Charley Mason of Bert.

"I haven't the least idea. I never knew Mr. Carford before this. I'll ask my father."

"Is that bill real?" asked one boy, referring to the money.

"It sure is," answered Bert, looking at it. "Come on to the drugstore and we'll spend it. That's what it's for."

"Going to treat Danny Rugg, and his crowd, too?" asked Frank Miller.

"Well, I guess Mr. Carford wanted this money to be spent on everyone on the hill, so it includes Danny," answered Bert slowly.

But Danny and his particular friends held back from Bert, and did not share in the treat. Probably Danny did not want to come too close to Bert after the attempt made to get Freddie's sled.

The excitement caused by the runaway was over now. Bert got back his sled and, as interest in coasting had waned at the prospect of hot chocolate sodas, the crowd of boys and girls trooped from the hill and started toward town, where there was a favorite drugstore.

Standing about the soda counter the boys and girls discussed the recent happening.

"What did you think, Nan, when you saw the team coming?" asked Grace Lavine.

"I really don't know what I did think," answered Nan.

"Weren't you awfully frightened?" inquired Nellie Parks.

"Oh, I suppose I was. But I hoped I could steer out of the way, and I remember hoping that Flossie and Freddie were in a safe place."

"Oh, we were all right," said Freddie quickly. "Flossie and I were watching the horses. This chocolate is awful good!" he added with a sigh. "Is there any money left, Bert?"

"Yes, a little," answered his brother. "But you have had your share."

"Oh, if there is any left let him and Flossie have it," suggested Grace. "They're the smallest ones here."

"Yes, do," urged Nellie, and as several others agreed that this was the thing to do, the two little Bobbsey twins each had another cup of chocolate.

"Though Freddie has almost as much outside his mouth as inside it," said Nan, with a laugh.

Then the merry party of boys and girls trooped homeward, Bert and Nan thinking on the way of the strange words of Mr. Carford and wondering what he meant by them.

Several of the older boys who knew the old gentleman told something of him. He was a strange character, living in a fine old homestead. He was said to be queer on certain matters, but kind and good and quite charitable, especially at Christmastime, to the poor of that country neighborhood.

"We'll ask papa about him when we get home," said Bert. "Maybe he can explain it."

But when the Bobbsey twins reached their house they found that their father had suddenly been called away on a business trip to last for some days, and so they did not see him.

"I haven't the least idea what Mr. Carford meant," said Mrs. Bobbsey, when they had asked her. "I did not even know that your father knew him. I am sorry you children were in danger on the hill."

"Oh, it wasn't much, mother," said Bert quickly, for he feared if his parent grew too worried she might put a stop to the winter fun.

Supper was soon ready and then came a happy period before bedtime—that is, happy after lessons had been learned. Snoop the black cat and Snap the smart circus dog were allowed in the living room to do some of their tricks, Snoop having been taught a number while with the fat lady in the circus.

Bert fell asleep vainly wondering about the queer words of Mr. Carford, and he dreamed that he was sliding downhill on the back of a horse who turned somersaults every now and then into a bag of popcorn.

Coasting came to an end the next day, for there was a big snowstorm, and the hill would not be in good condition until the white flakes were packed hard on the slope. But there were other forms of sport—snowballing, the making of forts, snow houses, and snowmen, so that the Bobbseys and their friends were kept busy.

Then came a little thaw, and the snow was just soft enough to roll into big balls.

"It's just right for making a large fort!" exclaimed Danny Rugg one day, after school was out. "We'll roll up a lot of big balls, put them in lines on four sides and make a square fort. Then we'll choose sides and have a snow fight."

The other boys agreed to this, and soon Bert and the others, including Danny and his friends, were busily engaged. For the time being the hard feelings between Danny and Bert were forgotten.

The fort was finished, and there was a spirited snow battle about it, one side trying to capture it and the other trying to stop them. Bert's side managed to get into the fort, driving the others out.

"Oh, we'll beat you tomorrow!" taunted Danny, when the battle was over.

The next morning, when the children assembled at school, they saw a strange sight. On the front steps of the building was a great snowball, so large that it almost hid the door from sight. And working at it, trying to cut it away so that the entrance could be used, was the janitor. He was having hard work it seemed.

"Who did it?"

"Who put it there?"

"Say, it's frozen fast, too!"

"Somebody will get into trouble about this."

These were only a few of the things said when the children saw the big snowball on the school steps.

"It's frozen fast all right enough," said the janitor, grimly. "Whoever put it there poured water over it, and it's frozen so fast that I'll have to chop it away piece by piece. All day it will take me, too, and me with all the paths to clean!"

When the classes were assembled for the morning exercises Mr. Tetlow, the school principal, stepped to the edge of the platform, and said, "I presume you have all seen the big snowball on the front steps. Whoever put it there did a very wrong thing. I know several boys must have had a hand in it, for one could not do it alone. I will now give those who did it a chance to confess. If they will admit it, and apologize, I will let the matter drop. If not I will punish them severely. Now are you ready to tell, boys? I may say that I have a clue to at least one boy who had a hand in the trick."

Mr. Tetlow paused. There was silence in the room, and the boys looked one at the other. Who was guilty?

CHAPTER 4

THE ACCUSATION

FOR what seemed a long time Mr. Tetlow stood looking over the room full of pupils. One could have heard a pin drop, so quiet it was. The hard breathing of the boys and girls could be heard. From over in a corner where Danny Rugg sat, came a sound of whispering.

"Quiet!" commanded the principal sharply. "There must be no talking. I will wait one minute more for the guilty ones to acknowledge that they rolled the big snowball on the steps. Then, if they do not speak, I shall have something to say."

The minute ticked slowly off on the big clock. No one spoke. Bert glanced from side to side as he sat in his seat, wondering what would come next. Many others had the same thought.

"I see no one wished to take advantage of my offer," said Mr. Tetlow slowly. "Very well. You may all go to your classrooms, with the exception of Bert Bobbsey. I wish to see him in my office at once. Do you hear that, Bert?"

There was a gasp of astonishment, and all eyes were turned on Bert. He grew red in the face, and then pale. He could see Nan looking at him curiously, as did other girls. Bert was glad Flossie and Freddie were not in the room, for the kindergarten children did not assemble for morning exercises with the larger boys and girls. Flossie and Freddie might have been frightened at the solemn talk.

For a moment Bert could hardly believe what he had heard. He was wanted in Mr. Tetlow's office! It did not seem possible. And there was but one explanation of it. It must be in connection with the big snowball. And Bert knew he had had no hand in putting it on the school steps.

There was a buzz of talk, many whisperings, and someone spoke aloud. It sounded like Danny Rugg, but poor Bert was so confused at his own plight that he could not be sure.

"Silence!" commanded Mr. Tetlow, as the boys and girls marched to their various rooms. "Bert, you will wait for me in my office," he added. Poor Bert looked all around. He met many glances that were kind, and others, from Danny Rugg's friends, that were not. Nan waved her hand at her brother as she passed him, and Bert smiled at her. He made up his mind to be brave.

Bert went to the principal's office, and sat in a

chair. There was another boy there, who looked at Bert in a questioning manner.

"Are you here to get some writing paper, Bert?" asked the other boy. "Miss Kennedy sent me for some."

"No," answered Bert. "I only wish I was. I guess Mr. Tetlow thinks I had something to do with the big snowball."

"Did you?"

"I did not!" exclaimed Bert quickly.

The principal entered a little later, gave to the other boy the package of writing paper Miss Kennedy had sent for, and then sat down beside Bert.

"I am sorry to have to do this, Bert," he said, "but this is a serious matter and I must treat it seriously. Now again, I ask if you have anything to say to me? Perhaps you were too worried to stand up before the whole school."

"No, sir," answered Bert, "I don't know that I have anything to say, if you mean about the big snowball."

"Then you deny that you had anything to do with it?"

"Yes, sir. I never helped roll it on the steps."

"Do you know who did?"

"No, sir. I haven't the least idea."

"And you were not anywhere near it?"

"No, sir."

"Ahem! Let me ask you, have you a knife, Bert?"

Without thinking Bert's hand went to his pocket, and then, as he recalled something, his face turned red, and he said, "I have one, but I haven't got it now."

"Is this it?" asked Mr. Tetlow, suddenly holding one.

Bert did not need to give more than a single glance at it to know that it was his knife. It had his name on the handle and had been given him by his father at Christmas.

"Yes, that's mine," he said slowly.

"So I thought. And do you know where it was found, Bert?"

"No, Mr. Tetlow, I haven't any idea."

"Suppose I told you the janitor picked it up on the steps almost under the big snowball? If I tell you that, what have you to say?"

"Well, Mr. Tetlow, I'll have to say that I don't know anything about it. I didn't drop my knife there, I'm sure."

"Then someone else must have done it. Be careful now, Bert. I don't want to be hasty, but it looks to me very much as though you were one of the boys who had played this trick—a trick that has made considerable trouble. I am sure there must have been others with you, and I am almost positive that you had a hand in it.

"Now I am not going to ask you to tell tales against your companions. I don't believe in that sort of thing. But I am very sorry that you did not admit at first that you had a share in rolling the big ball. Very sorry, Bert."

"But, Mr. Tetlow, I didn't do it!" cried poor Bert, the tears coming into his eyes. "I don't know how my knife got there, but I do know I didn't help roll that ball. Please believe me, won't you?"

For a moment the principal was silent. Then he said slowly, "Bert, I would very much like to believe you, for I have always found you a good, manly, and upright boy. But the evidence is strong against you, I am sorry to say. And this trick was one I cannot easily overlook. Rolling the snowball on the steps was bad enough, but when the water was poured over it to freeze and become ice, making it so much harder to clean off, it made matters so much worse.

"Besides making a lot of work for the janitor, there was danger that some of the teachers might slip on the icy path and be injured. If your knife had only been found lying on top of the ice I might think you had come up merely to look at the big ball, and had dropped your property there. But the knife was found frozen fast, showing that it must have been dropped during the time the water was poured on the steps. So you see whoever left it there must have been on hand when the trick was played."

"That may be true, Mr. Tetlow!" cried Bert, "but I did not leave my knife there. I remember now—I can explain it! I couldn't think, at first, but I see it now."

"Very well," said Mr. Tetlow quietly, "I'll hear what you have to say, Bert."

CHAPTER 5

HOLIDAYS AT HAND

BERT Bobbsey was thinking rapidly. Something that he had nearly forgotten came suddenly to his mind, and he hoped it would clear him of the accusation.

What he saw that brought back to his mind something he had forgotten was the sight of an elderly gentleman now driving past the school in a sled. It was aged Mr. Carford, whose runaway team Bert had helped stop that day on the hill.

"Will you let me call in Mr. Carford?" asked Bert of the principal.

"Call in Mr. Carford?" repeated Mr. Tetlow in some surprise. "What for?"

"Because, sir," said Bert eagerly, "he saw me lend my knife to Jimmie Belton last night, and he can tell you that I went on home, leaving my knife with Jimmie."

"Ha! Do you mean to say that Jimmie dropped it in the ice on the school steps?"

"No, Mr. Tetlow, I don't mean to say that. But I can prove by Mr. Carford that I went home last night without my knife. Please call him in."

Bert thought of the strange old man who had made such an odd remark concerning the Bobbsey family. And Bert was determined to find out what it meant, but, as yet, he had had no chance, as his father was still away on a business trip.

"Very well, we shall see what Mr. Carford has to say," spoke the principal. "And I will have Jimmie Belton in also."

Mr. Tetlow pressed a bell button that called the janitor, and the latter, who was still chopping away at the frozen steps, came to see what was wanted.

"Please call to that old gentleman going past in the bobsled to come inside," said Mr. Tetlow. "He is Mr. Carford."

"Tell him Bert Bobbsey wants to see him," added the boy, amazed at his own boldness.

"Yes, you may do that," said Mr. Tetlow, as the janitor looked toward him. Somehow the principal was beginning to doubt Bert's guilt now.

From the office window Bert watched the janitor hail the aged man, who paused for a minute, and then, tying his team, came on toward the school. Bert's heart was lighter now. He was sure the old gentleman would bear out what he had said, and Bert felt he would be glad to do him a good turn in partial payment for what Bert and his chums had done in catching the runaways.

"Mr. Carford," began Mr. Tetlow, who knew the aged man slightly, "there has been trouble here, and Bert Bobbsey thinks perhaps you can help clear it up. So I have asked you to step in for a moment." Then he told about the big snowball, and mentioned how he had come to suspect Bert.

"But Bert tells me," went on Mr. Tetlow, "that you saw him lending his knife to Jimmie Belton last night. May I ask you, is that so?"

"Why, yes, it is," said the aged man slowly. "I'll tell you how it was." He nodded at Bert in a friendly way, and there was a twinkle in his deep-set eyes.

"It was just toward dusk last evening," went on Mr. Carford, "and I was on my way home to Newton. I'd been in town buying some supplies, and near the crossroads I met Bert and another boy."

"That was Jimmie," said Bert eagerly.

"Well, I heard you call him Jimmie—that's all I know," said Mr. Carford. "Bert was cutting a branch from a tree, and when I came up to them I offered them a ride as far as I was going. They got in, and Bert here was whittling away with his knife as he sat beside me. Yes, that's the knife," said Mr. Carford, as the principal showed it to him.

"I was making a ramrod for a toy spring gun I

have," explained Bert. "It shoots long sticks, like arrows, and I had lost one of my best ones, so on the way home I cut another. Then just before Mr. Carford gave us the ride, Jimmie came along and asked me to lend him my knife. I said I would as soon as I had finished making my arrow. I did finish it in the sled and I gave him my knife just before we got out."

Mr. Tetlow looked inquiringly at Mr. Carford, who nodded in answer.

"Yes," said the aged man, "that was the way of it. Bert did lend that other boy—Jimmie he called him—his knife. I saw the two boys separate and Jimmie carried off Bert's knife. But that's all I do know. The snowball business I have nothing to do with."

"No, I suppose not," said the principal slowly. "I am sorry now that I said what I did, Bert. But there still remains the question of how your knife got on the steps. Do you think Jimmie had a hand in putting the snowball there?"

"I don't know, Mr. Tetlow. I wouldn't like to say."

"No, of course not. I'll have Jimmie here." The principal called a messenger and sent him for Jimmie, who came to the office wondering what it was all about.

Without telling him what was wanted, Mr.

Tetlow asked Jimmie this question quickly: "What did you do with Bert's knife after he lent it to you last night?"

For a moment Jimmie was confused. A strange look came over his face. He clapped his hand to his pocket and exclaimed, "I–I lent it to Danny Rugg."

"Danny Rugg!" cried Bert.

"No, I didn't exactly lend it to Danny," explained Jimmie, "for I knew, Bert, that you and he weren't very friendly. But after you let me take it last night, to start making that sailboat I was telling you about, I forgot all about promising you that I'd bring it back after supper. Then Danny came over and he helped me with the boat. When he saw I had your knife, and when he heard me say I must take it back, he offered to leave it for you when he came past your house the next time."

"And did you give it to him?" asked the principal.

"Yes, I did," answered Jimmie. "I thought he would do as he said. He took the knife when he went home from my house."

"But he never gave it to me!" said Bert quickly.

"I am beginning to believe he did not," said the principal. "I think we will have Danny in here."

The bully came in rather defiant, and stared boldly around at those in the office. Mr. Tetlow resolved on a surprising plan.

"Danny," he said suddenly, "why did you put

Bert's knife on the step and let it freeze there to make it look as though Bert had helped place the snowball in front of the door? Why did you?"

"I–I–" stammered Danny, "I didn't–"

"Be careful now," warned the principal. "We have heard the whole story. Jimmie has told how you promised to leave the knife with Bert, but you did not."

Danny swallowed a lump in his throat. He was much confused, and finally he broke down and admitted that he had been present and had helped roll the snowball on the steps.

"But I wasn't the only one!" he exclaimed. "There was–"

"Tut! Tut!" exclaimed the principal. "I want no tale-bearing. I think those who did the trick will confess now, after I tell them what has happened. Danny, it was very wrong of you to play such a joke, but it was much worse to try to throw the blame on Bert by leaving his knife there."

"I–I didn't do it on purpose," said Danny. "The knife must have slipped out of my pocket." But no one believed that, for Danny was known to have a grudge against Bert, and that was reason enough for trying to throw the blame on our little hero.

But Bert was soon cleared, for, a little later, when Mr. Tetlow called the school together, saying that he had been mistaken in regard to Bert, and relating what had come out about the knife, several of the boys who, with Danny, had placed the big ball on the steps admitted their part in it.

They were all punished, but Danny most of all, for his mean act in trying to make it look as though Bert had done it.

"Well," said Mr. Carford, as he took his leave, having helped to prove Bert's innocence, "this time I have had a chance to do a Bobbsey a favor, in return for the one you did me, Bert."

"Yes, sir," answered Bert, not knowing what else to say. He was puzzling over what strange connection there might be between his family and Mr. Carford.

"Come up and see me sometime," said the aged man. "And bring your brother and sisters, Bert. I'll be glad to see them at my place. I'm going to stay home all this winter. I'm getting too old to go to Snow Lodge anymore."

Bert wondered what Snow Lodge was, but he did not like to ask.

Thus was cleared up the mystery of the big snowball, and Bert's many friends were as glad as he was himself that he had been found innocent.

There came more snowstorms, followed by freezing weather after a thaw, and the boys and girls had much fun on the ice, a number of skating races having been arranged among the school pupils.

The end of the midwinter term was approaching,

and the Christmas holidays would soon be at hand. Then would come a three-week vacation, and the Bobbsey twins were talking about how they could spend it.

"It's too cold to go to the seashore," said Nan with a shiver, as she looked out of the window over the snowy yard.

"And the country would be about the same," added Bert.

"Oh, it's lovely in the country during the winter, I think," said Nan.

"We could get up a circus in the barn, with Snoop and Snap," said Flossie, who was busy over a picture book.

"Then I'm going to be the ringmaster and crack a big whip and wear big boots!" cried Freddie.

"I do hope papa will be home for Christmas," sighed Nan, for Mr. Bobbsey's business trip, in relation to lumber matters, had kept him away from home longer than expected.

"I have good news for you, children," said Mrs. Bobbsey, coming into the room just then with a letter. "Your father is coming home tomorrow."

"Oh, how nice!" cried Nan.

"I hope he brings us something," said Freddie.

"I'll have a chance to ask him about Mr. Carford," thought Bert. "I wonder what that old man meant by his strange words?"

CHAPTER 6

A VISIT TO MR. CARFORD

"FREDDIE, what in the world are you doing?"

"Flossie! Oh dear! You children! You have the place all upset!"

Mrs. Bobbsey, who had come into the big living room to see the two younger twins engaged in some strange proceedings, paused at the doorway to look on. Indeed the place was upset, for the chairs had been dragged out from against the walls and from corners to be placed in a row before a large sofa. From one corner of this to a side wall was stretched a sheet, and in another corner, in a pen made of chairs, could be seen the wagging tail of Snap, the trick dog.

"What in the world are you doing?" asked Mrs. Bobbsey. "Oh, dear, how I do dread a rainy day!" For it was pouring outside, and the older and the younger twins had to stay indoors.

"We're playing circus," explained Freddie gravely, as he peered between the "bars" of the cage made of chairs. "Snap is a lion," went on the little fellow. "Growl, Snap!"

And Snap, always ready to have fun, growled and barked to satisfy the most exacting circus lover.

"Oh, dear!" cried Mrs. Bobbsey. "I'll never get this room straightened out again."

"Oh, we'll fix it, mamma, after the circus," said Flossie sweetly. "Sit down and see the show. I'll make Snoop do some of the tricks the fat circus lady taught her," and Flossie lifting up one corner of the sheet, showed the black cat curled up on a cushion, while behind her, tied by one leg, was Downy the pet duck.

"This was going to be the happy family cage," explained Flossie, "only when we had Snap in here he kept playing with Downy. Downy quacked, and that made Snoop nervous so we couldn't do it very well."

"So we made Snap the lion, and part of the time he's going to be the tiger," said Freddie. "Dinah is going to give us some bluing that she uses on the clothes, and I'm going to paint stripes on Snap."

"Don't you dare do it," said Mrs. Bobbsey. "The idea of painting blue stripes on poor Snap! Whoever heard of a blue-striped tiger?" and she tried hard not to laugh.

"Well, this is a new kind," said Freddie. "Sit down, mamma, and we'll make Snoop do a trick for you. Make her chase her tail, Flossie."

"No, I'll make her walk a tightrope," said the little girl. "That's more of a trick."

Flossie got her jumping rope, which she had little use for now, and tied it from the back of one chair to the back of another one placed some distance away. Then she pulled the rope tight between them, and, taking Snoop up in her arms, placed the cat carefully on the stretched rope.

Snoop stood still for a minute, meowing a little and waving her tail back and forth. Poor Snoop! The black cat did not like to do tricks as well as did Snap. No cats do. But Snap, when he saw what was going on, was eager to show off what he could do.

He leaped about in his chair "cage," barking loudly, much to the delight of Freddie who liked to hear the "lion" roar.

"Go on, Snoop!" called the twins, and gave the cat a gentle shove. Then Snoop did really walk across the rope, for it was almost as easy as walking the back fence, which Snoop had often done. Only the rope was not as steady as the fence. But the fat circus lady had trained the black cat well, and Snoop performed the trick to the delight of the children.

"That is very good," said Mrs. Bobbsey. "Oh, see! Snap is turning a somersault in his cage. Poor dog, let him out, Freddie, won't you?"

"He isn't a dog—he's a lion," insisted the little boy. "I dassen't let out a lion, or he might bite you."

But Snap had no idea of playing the lion all the while. Suddenly Downy, the duck, with a loud quack, got her leg loose from the string and flew out across the room. This so surprised Snoop, who had started back over the tightrope, that he fell off with a cry of alarm.

This was too much for Snap, who evidently did not think he was having his share of the fun. With a loud bark and a rush he burst from his cage of chairs, intent on playing with Snoop, for he and the cat were great friends.

Just at that moment fat Dinah, the family cook, came into the room to ask Mrs. Bobbsey something. Snoop, seeing the open door, and being tired of doing tricks for the children, made a dash to get out, darting under Dinah's skirts.

Snap, thinking this was part of the game, rushed after his friend the cat, but when he tried to dive underneath Dinah's dress there was an accident.

He knocked the feet from under the plump cook, and she sat down on the floor with a force that jarred the whole house, just missing sitting on Snap.

"What is the matter?" cried Dinah. "Is it an earthquake, Mrs. Bobbsey?"

"I don't know, Dinah!" exclaimed Mrs. Bobbsey, wanting to laugh, and yet not wishing to hurt Dinah's feelings. "The children said it was a circus, I believe. Here, Snap!" she called, as the dog rushed on after Snoop.

Just then Downy, the duck, sailed back across the room, and lighted squarely on Dinah's head, where the fowl perched "honking" loudly.

"More trouble!" exclaimed Dinah.

Flossie and Freddie were so surprised at the sudden ending of their circus that they did not know what to do. Then they both raced to capture the duck from Dinah's hair.

"Are you hurt, Dinah?" asked Flossie. "If you are you can come to our circus for nothing; can't she, Freddie?"

"Yes," he answered, "only we haven't got a circus now. It's all gone except Downy."

"Well, I think you have played enough circus for today," said Mrs. Bobbsey. "Straighten up the room now, and have some other kind of fun."

The dog and cat, satisfied to get out of their cages, had gone to the kitchen, where they could generally find something good to eat. Then Flossie and Freddie were kept busy putting back the chairs, and setting the room in order.

It was a day or so after the return of Mr. Bobbsey from his business trip, and though Bert had asked his father about Mr. Carford, the lumber dealer had not yet had time to give any explanation.

"It is quite a little story," he said. "I'll tell you about it some time, Bert. But now I have a lot of back work to catch up with, on account of being away so long, and I'll have to go to the office early, and I'll be late getting home."

So the little incident had not yet been explained. The Christmas holidays were drawing nearer, and there were busy times in the Bobbsey household. Flossie and Freddie were expecting a visit from Santa Claus, and they wrote many letters to the dear old saint, telling what they wished to receive.

"But have you thought of what you are going to *give*?" asked Mrs. Bobbsey one day, a short time before Christmas. "It is more fun to give things than it is to get them, you know."

"Is it?" asked Flossie, who had never heard of it in that way before.

"Indeed it is," said Mrs. Bobbsey. "You just try it. If you have any toys you don't care for anymore, or even some that you do, and wish to give away, or books or other playthings, and if you will gather them up, I'll see that they are given to some poor children who may not have a very good Christmas."

The smaller twins thought this would be very

nice, and they were soon busy over their possessions. Bert and Nan heard what was going on and they insisted on giving their share also, so that quite a box full of really good toys were collected.

A day or so later, when the whether had cleared, Bert came in from coasting, and said, "Mother, couldn't Nan and I take a ride over to Mr. Carford's house? He is out in front in his sled, and he says he'll bring us back before dark. May we go?"

"Why, I guess so," said Mrs. Bobbsey, slowly. "I don't believe your father would object. But wrap up well, for it is chilly."

"And can't we go, too?" begged Flossie.

"Yes, we want to," added Freddie. "Please, mamma!"

"Well, I guess so," agreed Mrs. Bobbsey. "Will you look after them, Bert and Nan?"

"Oh, yes," promised the two older twins, while Bert explained that he had met Mr. Carford, who was on his way home from the store, and had been given a ride. The invitation had followed.

"I'll take good care of them, Mrs. Bobbsey," said the elderly gentleman, as Mrs. Bobbsey went out to tuck in Flossie and Freddie. "I've got to run into Newton and back again this afternoon, so I thought they'd like the ride."

"Indeed it is very kind of you," said the children's mother. "I hope they will be no trouble."

"Of course they won't. Remember me to Mr. Bobbsey when he comes home. Ask him to come and see me when he has time. I want to talk to him about a certain matter."

"All right," said Mrs. Bobbsey, and Bert wondered if it had to do with the secret.

The drive out to Newton, which was a few miles from Lakeport, was much enjoyed by the Bobbsey twins. The speedy horses pulled the sled over the white snow, the jingle of the strings of bells around them mingling with other musical chimes on sleds that they met, or passed.

They saw Danny Rugg out driving with his mother in a stylish cutter, and Danny rather "turned up his nose" at the old bobsled in which the Bobbseys were riding. But Bert and his sisters and brother did not mind that. They were having a good time.

"Here we are!" called Mr. Carford after a fine ride. "Come in and get warm. I guess my sister has a few cookies left," for a maiden sister kept house for the old gentleman.

Into the big old-fashioned farmhouse the children tramped, to be met by a motherly-looking woman, who helped them brush the snow from their feet. Then she bustled about and brought in a big pitcher of milk, a plateful of molasses cookies, and some glasses. The children's eyes sparkled at the sight of this fine lunch.

"There you are!" cried Mr. Carford heartily, as he passed around the good things. "Eat as much as is good for you. I've got to go out to the barn for a while. Emma," he asked his sister, "have you got any more packages made up?"

"James Carford, are you going to give away more stuff?" demanded his sister. "Why, you'll be in the poorhouse, first thing you know."

"Oh, I guess not," he said with a laugh. "We can afford it, and there's many who can't. It's going to be a hard winter on the poor. Put up a few more packages, and I'll tie up some bags of potatoes!"

"I never saw such a man—never in all my born days!" exclaimed Miss Carford, shaking her head. "He'd give away the roof over us if I didn't watch him."

"What is he doing?" asked Bert.

"Oh, the same as he does every Christmas," said the sister-housekeeper. "He makes up packages, bundles, baskets, and bags of things to eat, and gives them to all the poor families he can hear of. He was poor once himself, you know, and he never can forget it."

"He is very kind," said Nan, in a low voice.

"Yes, he is that," agreed Miss Carford, "and I suppose I oughtn't to find fault. But he does give away an awful lot."

She went out to look after matters in the kitchen, leaving the children to eat their lunch of milk and cookies alone for a few minutes. Presently Mr. Carford came back, stamping the snow from his boots.

"Ha!" he cried, as he went close to the stove to warm his hands. "This reminds me of the winters I used to spend at Snow Lodge on Lake Metoka. Were you ever up there?" and he looked at Bert.

"No, sir."

"Ha! I thought not. It's a fine place. But I don't go there anymore—never anymore," and he shook his head sadly.

"Did it burn down?" asked Freddie, who was always interested in fires and firemen. "Couldn't they put it out?"

"No, Freddie, it didn't burn down," said Mr. Carford. "Sometimes I almost wish it had—before my trouble happened," he added slowly. "Yes, I almost wish it had. But Snow Lodge still stands, though I haven't been near it for some years. I couldn't go. No, I couldn't go," and he shook his head sadly. "I just couldn't go."

The Bobbsey children did not know what to think. Mr. Carford seemed very sad. Suddenly he turned away from the fire that blazed on the hearth, and asked, "Did I ever tell you about Snow Lodge?"

"No," said Bert softly.

"Then I will," went on the aged man. "I don't tell many, but I will you. And maybe you could make some use of the place now that the holidays are here. I used to spend all my Christmas holidays there, but I don't anymore. Never anymore. But I'll tell you about it," and he settled himself more comfortably in the big chair.

CHAPTER 7

THE STORY OF SNOW LODGE

"WHEN I was a boy," began Mr. Carford after a pause, during which he looked into the blazing fire, "I lived on a farm, and I had to work very hard."

"We were on a farm once, weren't we, Flossie?" interrupted Freddie.

"Hush, dear," said Nan in a low voice. "Listen to Mr. Carford's story."

"That isn't a story," insisted Flossie. "He didn't begin it right. He must say: 'Once upon a time, a good many years ago—!'"

Mr. Carford laughed.

"So I should, my dear!" he exclaimed. "It's been so long since I've told a story to little folks that I've forgotten how, I guess.

"So I'll begin over again. Once upon a time, a good many years ago, I was a little boy and I lived on a farm. I guess it must have been the same sort of a farm you and Flossie went to, Freddie, for we had cows and horses and pigs and chickens and sheep. There was lots of work, and, as my father was not rich, I had to help as soon as I got old enough.

"But, for all that, I had good times. I thought so then and, though I'm an old man now, I still think so. But the good times did not last long enough. I wish I could go back to them.

"But I stayed on the farm a good many years, with my brothers and sisters, and finally when I grew up, and thought I was big enough to start to work for myself, I ran away."

"Did you—did you get lost?" asked Flossie, with her eyes wide open, staring at Mr. Carford.

"No, my dear, I didn't exactly get lost. But I thought there was easier work than living on a farm, so, instead of staying and helping my father, as I think now I should have done, I ran away to a big city. I wanted to be dressed up, and wear a white collar instead of overalls and a jumper.

"But I found that life in the city, instead of being easier than on the farm, was harder, especially as I didn't know much about it. Many a time I wished I was back with my father but I was too proud to admit that I had made a mistake. So I kept on working in the city, and finally I began to forget all about the farm.

"I won't make this story too long, for you might

get tired of it," said Mr. Carford, as he got up to put a log on the fire.

"Oh, we like stories, don't we, Freddie?" said Flossie.

"Yes," said Freddie softly.

"I know, my dear," said the old man kindly, "but I am afraid you wouldn't like my kind. Anyhow I kept on working in the city—in one city after another—until I became successful and then, in time, I got rich."

"Rich!" cried Freddie. "Very rich?" and his big eyes opened wide.

"Freddie!" cautioned Nan, with a sharp look.

"Oh, I don't mind!" laughed Mr. Carford. "Yes, I got quite rich, and then I thought it was time to go back to the old farm and see my father. My mother had died before I went away. Maybe if she had lived I wouldn't have gone. And then I began to find out that life wasn't all happiness just because you had money.

"My father had died too, and the old farm had been sold. My brothers and sisters had gone—some were married and some had died. I found I was a lonesome old man, with few friends and hardly any relatives left. I had been too busy getting rich, you see, to take time to make friends.

"Well, I didn't know what to do. All the while, you understand, I had been counting on going back to the farm, with a lot of money, and saying to my father: 'Now, daddy, you've worked hard enough. You can stop now, and have happiness the rest of your life.' But you see my father wasn't there. I was too late.

"So I made up my mind the best thing I could do was to buy back the old farm, and spend the rest of my days there, for the sake of old times. Well, I did buy the place, and I named it 'Snow Lodge,' for there used to be lots of snow there in the winter-time. I fixed the old house all over new, put in a furnace and other things to make it comfortable, and I lived there for some time.

"I heard from some of my brothers and sisters who had also gone away from the farm, and one of my sisters, who had married a man named Burdock, had become very poor. Her husband had died, and she was very sick. I brought her to Snow Lodge to live with me, and her son, Henry, a fine lad, came along.

"My poor sister did not live very long, and when she died I took Henry Burdock to live with me. I felt toward him as toward a son, and for years we stayed in Snow Lodge together.

"Then I bought this place, and we used to spend part of the year here and part of it at Snow Lodge. It was a fine place winter or summer, Snow Lodge was."

Mr. Carford became silent and looked again into the glowing logs on the hearth.

"Don't you go to Snow Lodge anymore?" asked Nan in a low voice.

"No," replied the old man. "Never anymore. Not—not since Henry went away," and he seemed to be in pain. "I have never gone there since Henry went away," he added, "though the place is well kept up, and it is ready to live in this minutc."

"Did your nephew Henry run away, as you did?" asked Bert.

"No—not exactly," was the reply. "I don't like to talk about that part of it. I like to think of Snow Lodge on the shore of the lake as a place where I lived when I was a boy.

"Oh, it's just fine there!" went on Mr. Carford. "In summer the grass is so green, and you can sit on the porch and look down at the lake. In the winter, when the lake is frozen over, there is skating and ice-boating on it, and you can fish through the ice. And such hills as there are to coast down! And such valleys filled with snow! Sometimes it seems as if the whole house would be covered with the white flakes.

"But you can always keep warm in Snow Lodge, for there are big fireplaces, as well as the furnace, and there is plenty of wood. Many times I've had a notion to go back there, but somehow I couldn't, since—since Henry went away. So I came here to live with my other sister, and here I guess I'll stay the rest of my life. Snow Lodge is shut up, and I guess it always will be."

Mr. Carford sighed, and kept looking at the fire. Nan thought what a pity it was that Snow Lodge could not be used, while Bert wondered what had happened between Henry Burdock and his uncle, Mr. Carford, that caused Henry to go away. Also Bert wondered if Mr. Carford would explain his strange remark, made at the time the runaway horses were caught. But the aged man seemed to have forgotten it.

"Yes, Snow Lodge is closed up," said Mr. Carford. "I don't suppose it will ever be used again. But I've told you the story of it, and I'm afraid I've tired you."

"No you haven't," said Nan. "We enjoyed it very much."

"That's right!" exclaimed Bert.

"Did—did you ever see any bears there?" asked Freddie, "any real big bears?"

"Or tigers—or—or elephants?" asked Flossie, not to let her brother get ahead of her in asking questions.

"Huh! Elephants don't grow here—only bears," said Freddie.

"No, I never saw anything bigger than foxes,"

said Mr. Carford with a laugh. "Snow Lodge isn't very far from here, you know, so you have the same kind of animals there that you have here. Only there are more woods at Snow Lodge.

"But I must be getting back with you youngsters. It is getting late and your folks may worry about you. I'll bring the sled around, and my sister Emma can tuck you in. Then I'll get you home, and see to my Christmas packages. It's going to be a hard winter on the poor."

"We give the poor people something," said Freddie. "At school we all brought something just before vacation, and Mr. Tetlow is going to give it to all the poor people."

"That was at Thanksgiving, dear," said Nan.

"Well, maybe they've got some left for Christmas," said Freddie, as the others laughed.

"That's right—try and make other people happy, little man," said Mr. Carford, patting Freddie's head.

The big sled with the horses and their jingling bells was soon at the door. Miss Carford had warmed some bricks to put down in the straw to keep the children's feet warm, and soon, cozily wrapped up, they were on their way home.

CHAPTER 8

A KIND OFFER

"NAN!" called Freddie from under a big fur robe, as he sat in the warm straw of Mr. Carford's sled next to his sister.

"Yes, what is it?" asked Nan, bending over him to look at his face in the gathering dusk of the winter afternoon. "Are you warm enough, Freddie?"

"Yes, I'm as warm as the toast Dinah makes for breakfast. But say, I want to ask you—do you think we'll meet Santa Claus before we get home?"

"No, Freddie. The idea! What makes you think that?"

"Well, it's near Christmas, and we're out in a sled, and he goes out in a sled, only with reindeers of course, and—"

Freddie's voice trailed off sleepily. In fact he had aroused himself from almost a nap to ask Nan the question. Flossie, warmly wrapped up, was already slumbering in Bert's arms.

"No, I don't believe we'll meet Santa Claus this

trip," said Nan. "He is only supposed to travel at night, you know, Freddie."

"That's so. Well, if we do meet him, and I'm asleep, will you wake me up?"

"Yes, Freddie," promised his sister and she looked across at Bert and smiled. The two younger twins were soon both soundly slumbering, for being out in the cold air and wind does seem to make one sleepy when, later on, one gets warm and comfortable.

Mr. Carford sat up on the seat in front driving the sturdy horses, while the string of bells around them jingled at every step.

"Wasn't that a queer story of Snow Lodge?" asked Nan of Bert in a low voice.

"It surely was," he replied. "It seems too bad to have the place all shut up, with no one to use it this winter. It would be just great, I think, if we could go up there for the Christmas holidays. We could go up right after Christmas, and not come back until the middle of January, for school doesn't open again until then. Wouldn't it be great!"

"Fine!" agreed Nan. "But I don't s'pose we could. Mr. Carford doesn't want Snow Lodge used, I guess. But he gave us a good time at his house."

"Indeed he did," agreed Bert.

On glided the sled, the bells making merry music. A light snowfall began, and Mr. Carford urged the horses to go at a faster speed, for he wanted to get back home before the storm broke.

"Wake up, Freddie!"

"Wake up, Flossie!"

Nan and Bert gently shook their little brother and sister to arouse them. The sled had stopped in front of the Bobbsey home.

"Is it—is it morning?" asked Flossie, as she rubbed her eyes.

"Did Santa Claus come?" demanded Freddie, trying to wiggle out of Bert's arms.

"Not yet," laughed Mr. Carford. "But I think he soon will be here. Can you manage them, Nan—Bert?" he asked.

"Oh, yes, we often carry them," replied Nan. "They'll soon be wide awake again, and they won't want to go to sleep until late tonight, on account of the nap they've had."

Mrs. Bobbsey was at the door waiting for the children. Flossie and Freddie soon roused up enough to walk in.

"Won't you come in?" asked Mrs. Bobbsey of Mr. Carford. "I can give you a cup of tea. Mr. Bobbsey just came home. Perhaps you'd like to say 'how-d'ye-do.' "

"Thanks, I'll come in for just a minute," was the answer. "Then I must be getting back before the storm breaks. And I'll tie my horses, too. I can't risk another runaway," Mr. Carford said with a smile at Bert.

Mr. Bobbsey greeted the caller cordially, and the children were soon telling their parents of the nice visit they had had.

"And Miss Carford can make almost as good cookies as Dinah!" cried Freddie.

"Ha! Ha!" laughed Mr. Carford. "I'll have to tell my sister that. She'll be real proud."

Bert, looking from his father to Mr. Carford, wondered what could have once taken place between the two men. That there was some sort of secret he felt sure, and up to now there had been no explanation of the strange words used by the aged man at the time Bert and the others caught the runaways.

"I haven't seen you in some time, Mr. Bobbsey," said Mr. Carford, after they had talked about the weather.

"No, I've been very busy, and I suppose you have also. Have you been at Snow Lodge lately?"

"No, and I don't expect to set foot in the place again. I guess you know why. And I want to say now, that though I was rather cross with you when you tried to get me to change my mind about that matter some time ago, I want to say that I'm sorry for it. I realize that you did it for the best."

"Yes," said Mr. Bobbsey, "I did, but I know how

you felt about it. I believed then, and I believe now, that you made a mistake about your nephew Henry."

"No, I don't think I did," was the slow reply. "I am afraid Henry is a bad young man. I don't want to see him again, nor Snow Lodge either. But I'm glad you tried to help me. However, I have come about a different matter now. How would you and your family like to spend the winter there? How would a vacation at Snow Lodge suit you?"

No one spoke for a few seconds. All were surprised at the kind offer made by Mr. Carford.

"A vacation at Snow Lodge!" said Mr. Bobbsey slowly.

"Do you mean it, Mr. Carford?" asked Mrs. Bobbsey.

"I certainly do," was the answer. "I have told your youngsters something about Snow Lodge, and they seemed to like the place. I heard them talking among themselves on the way back here, how they'd like to go there.

"Oh, that's all right—no harm done!" exclaimed Mr. Carford, as he looked at the blushing faces of Nan and Bert. "I'm glad I did overhear what you were saying. It is a shame to keep that place locked up, and I'm just beginning to realize it.

"I don't want to go there myself, but that's no reason why others shouldn't. So, Mr. Bobbsey, if you like, you can take your whole family up there to Snow Lodge near the lake and in the woods, and stay as long as you like. Here are the keys!" and Mr. Carford tossed a jingling bunch on the table.

CHAPTER 9

MR. BOBBSEY'S STORY

"SNOW Lodge! Oh, Papa, could we go there?" cried Flossie, now wide awake.

"What fun we could have!" exclaimed Freddie, whose eyes were now as wide open as ever they had been.

Bert and Nan said little, but there was a look of pleased anticipation on their faces. They, too, realized what fun they could have in a big old-fashioned farmhouse in winter, particularly when the building was refitted with a furnace, and had big fireplaces in it.

And Bert was wondering, more than ever, what strange reason Mr. Carford could have for not wanting to go back to lovely Snow Lodge.

"Say we can go, Daddy!" pleaded the two smaller twins, as they tried to get into their father's lap.

"Well," said Mr. Bobbsey slowly, "this is certainly very kind of you, Mr. Carford, but I am not sure I can accept it. I am very much obliged to you, however—"

"Accept! Of course you can accept!" exclaimed the aged man. "There's no reason why you and your family shouldn't have a holiday vacation at Snow Lodge. The place has been closed up a long time, but a day or so with a good fire in it would make it as warm as toast. I know, for I've been there on the coldest winter days. Now you just plan to go up there with the wife and children, and have a good time. It might as well be used as to stand idle and vacant, as it is."

"What do you say, Mother?" and Mr. Bobbsey looked at his wife. "Shall we go to Snow Lodge?"

"The children would like it," said Mrs. Bobbsey slowly.

"Like it! I should say we would!" cried Nan. "I can take some pictures of the birds with my new camera—the one I am going to get for Christmas," she added with a smile.

"Oh ho! So you are going to have a camera for Christmas, are you?" laughed her father.

"I—I hope so," she replied.

"And I can build a snow house and live in it like the Eskimos," added Bert.

"Then I'm going to live with you!" cried Freddie. "Please go to Snow Lodge, mamma!"

"Yes, take the youngsters up," urged Mr.

Carford. "At least don't decide against it now. I'll leave the keys with you, and you can go any time you like. I don't suppose it will be until after Christmas, though, for Santa Claus might not be able to get up there," and he pinched Freddie's fat cheek.

"No, don't go until after Santa Claus has been here," urged Flossie seriously, and her mother laughed.

"Well, I must be going, anyhow," said Mr. Carford, after a pause. "It will be dark before I get back, and the storm seems to be coming up quickly. Emma will worry, I'm afraid. Now you just think it over about Snow Lodge," he concluded, "and I guess you will go, Mr. Bobbsey. You know my reasons for not wanting to set foot in the place, so I don't need to tell you.

"Now, good-bye. Go to Snow Lodge, and have a good time, and when you come back, children, tell me all about it. If I can't go there at least I like to hear about the place."

Mr. Carford went out to his team, through the now driving snow. He little realized what a joyful story the Bobbsey twins were to bring back to him from Snow Lodge, nor how it was to change his feeling in regard to his boyhood home.

"Papa," said Bert soberly, after the visitor had gone, leaving the keys of Snow Lodge behind him, "what is the secret about Mr. Carford and that winter place? And you're mixed up in it, I'm sure."

"What makes you sure, Bert?"

"Well, I've been thinking so ever since that day I helped to catch his runaway horses, and he said this was the second time a Bobbsey had tried to do him a favor."

"Had your favor anything to do with Snow Lodge, Papa?" asked Nan, as she put her arms about his neck.

"Well, yes, daughter, in a way. And, since Mr. Carford had told you part of the story, I may as well tell you the other half, I suppose."

"Oh, another story!" cried Flossie, in delight.

"Yes, we must be quiet and listen," said Freddie, as he drew up a stool close to his father.

"It isn't a very nice sort of story," went on Mr. Bobbsey. "In fact it is rather sad. But I'll tell it to you, anyhow. Did Mr. Carford tell you about when he was a boy?"

"Yes, and how he went away and came back rich and found all his folks gone and the farm sold," said Nan.

"Yes. Well, I guess he told you then how he took his nephew, Henry Burdock, to live with him. He loved Henry almost as if he were his own son, and did everything for him. In fact he planned to leave him all his money. Then came a quarrel."

"What about?" asked Bert softly.

"Over some money. Henry was a young man who liked to spend considerable, and, though he was not bad he was different from the country boys. Mr. Carford gave him plenty of spending money, however, and did not ask him what became of it.

"Then, one day, a large sum of money was missing from Snow Lodge. Mr. Carford accused Henry of taking it, and Henry said he had seen nothing of it. Then came a quarrel, and Mr. Carford, in a fit of temper, drove Henry away from Snow Lodge. There were bitter words on both sides, and after that Mr. Carford closed up the place, and has not been near it since. That is the part of the story Mr. Carford did not tell you."

"But where do you come in, Daddy?" asked Nan. "Did you find the missing money?"

"No, Nan, though I wish I had. But I was sure Henry had not taken it, and I tried to make Mr. Carford believe so. That is what he meant by me trying to do him a favor. But he would not have it so, and, for a time, he had some feeling against me. But it passed away, for he realized that I was trying to help him.

"But since then Mr. Carford and his nephew have not spoken. As I said, Mr. Carford drove the young man away from Snow Lodge. It was in a raging storm and Henry might have been frozen, only

I found him and took him to a hotel. I helped look after him until he could get a start. It was a very sad affair, and it has spoiled Mr. Carford's life, for he loved Henry very much."

"And did Henry really take the money?" asked Freddie. "That was wicked, I think."

"You must not say so, Freddie," spoke Mr. Bobbsey. "We do not know that Henry did take it. No one knows. It is a mystery. I, myself feel sure that Henry did not, but I cannot prove that he did not take it. His uncle believes that he did. At any rate the money disappeared."

"And where was it when Mr. Carford last saw it?" asked Nan.

"Mr. Carford left it on the mantelpiece in the big living room of Snow Lodge," said Mr. Bobbsey. "Henry was the only other person besides himself who was in the room, and in some way the money was taken. I even went so far as to have a man from the police station look all over the house, hoping he could find the roll of bills somewhere, but it did not come to light. And so, ever since, there has been a bad feeling between Henry and his uncle."

"What does Henry Burdock do now?" asked Bert.

"He roams about the woods, as a sort of guide and hunter. Sometimes, I am told, he comes close to Snow Lodge and looks down on it from a distant hill, thinking of the happy days he spent there."

"Maybe we'll see him when we go up," said Freddie. "If I do I'll give him all the money in my bank so he can be friends with his uncle again."

"No, Freddie," said Mrs. Bobbsey solemnly. "You must not speak of what you have just heard. It is a sad story, and is best forgotten. Both Mr. Carford and Henry feel bad enough about it, so it will be best not to mention it. Just forget all about it if we go to Snow Lodge."

"But we are going, aren't we, Papa?" asked Bert. "The trip to the woods would do us all good."

"Well, I think we might take advantage of Mr. Carford's kind offer," said Mr. Bobbsey. "Yes, we'll plan to go to Snow Lodge!"

"Hurrah!" cried Nan and Bert, grasping each other by the hands and swinging around in a sort of waltz.

"Can we take our sleds?" asked Flossie.

"I'm going to take my skates. Maybe I'll skate all the way there—I could—on the lake!" exclaimed Freddie, and he wondered why the others laughed.

"Well, we'll make our plans later," said Mrs. Bobbsey. "Now, children, we'll have an early supper and then you must all get to bed. Christmas will come so much earlier if you go to sleep now."

"Oh, jolly Christmas!" cried Nan. "I can hardly wait!"

CHAPTER 10

UNWELCOME NEWS

"MERRY Christmas!"

"Merry Christmas to everybody!"

"Oh, Christmas is here! I wonder what I got?"

"I'm going to get up and see!"

The Bobbsey twins were calling to one another from their rooms, and papa and mamma Bobbsey were replying to their children's happy greetings. It was Flossie who had made the exclamation about wondering what Santa Claus had brought her, and it was Freddie who declared he was going to get up to see.

Soon the patter of bare feet announced that the two younger twins were scampering downstairs.

"You must put on your dressing gowns and slippers, my dears!" called Mrs. Bobbsey. "You'll take cold. Nan, look after them, will you?"

"Yes, mother, in just a minute. As soon as I can find my own things," and Nan got out of bed. She and Bert were not in so much of a hurry as Flossie and Freddie for they were getting older, and though Christmas was still a source of great joy to them they were not so anxious to see what gifts they had. Still Nan was eager to know if her camera had come.

From the parlor below came cries, shouts and peals of delighted and surprised laughter as Flossie and Freddie discovered their different gifts.

"Look at my book!" cried Flossie. "And a doll—a doll that you can wind up, and she walks and says 'mamma.' Look, Freddie!" and the little girl started the doll off across the room.

"Pooh! Look at what I got!" cried Freddie. "It's a fire engine, and it squirts real water. I'm going to put some in it, and play fire."

He started for the kitchen with his toy, but Nan caught him.

"Not just yet, little Fat Fireman," she said with a laugh, as she took him up in her arms. "You can't splash in the cold water until you have more clothes on. Get dressed and then you may play with your toys."

"All right!" answered Freddie. "Oh, look, I've got a wind-up steamboat, too. Oh, let me down so I can look at it, Nan! Now please do!"

Nan saw a pile of her own gifts so she set Freddie down for a moment, intending to carry him up stairs a little later. She had wrapped a robe about Flossie, who was contentedly playing with her newest doll and looking at her other presents. Santa Claus had been kind to the Bobbsey twins that Christmas.

Bert, big boy though he thought himself getting to be, could no longer resist the temptation to come down in his bathrobe to see what he had received, and a little later Dinah, roused earlier than usual by the joyous shouts of the children, camc in too.

"Oh, Dinah! Dinah! Look what you got!" cried Flossie. "Your things are all here on this chair," and the little girl led the fat cook over toward it.

"Things for me? I don't get any presents from Santa!" she said, laughing so that she shook all over.

"Yes, you do get a Christmas, Dinah. Look here!" and Flossie showed where there were some presents for the cook: large aprons, warm shoes, an umbrella, and a bright shawl that Dinah had been wanting for a long time.

"What? All for me?" asked the surprised cook. "I guess ole Santa Claus has made a mistake!"

"No, there's no mistake! See, your name is right here!" insisted Flossie. She led the cook over to the chair where the presents were piled. There was no doubt of it, they were for Dinah, and near them was another chair containing gifts for her husband, Sam. He would not be in until later, however. But

Dinah saw a pair of rubber boots that would be very useful in the deep snow, and there were other fine presents for Sam.

Bert and Nan were now looking at their things, and Mr. and Mrs. Bobbsey could be heard moving around upstairs, having decided that it was useless to lie in bed any longer now that the children were up.

"Come, come, Flossie and Freddie!" called Mrs. Bobbsey. "You must get dressed and then you can play as much as you like. I don't want you to get cold. If you do you can't go to Snow Lodge, remember!"

This was enough to cause the small Bobbseys to scamper upstairs. Flossie carried her doll with her, and Freddie took along his fire engine, for that was the gift he had most wanted, and for which he had begged and pleaded for weeks before Christmas.

Feeling that a little liberty might be allowed on this day, Mrs. Bobbsey did not insist on the younger children dressing completely until after breakfast, so in their warm robes and slippers Flossie and Freddie were soon again examining their toys, discovering new delights every few minutes.

Nan was busy inspecting her camera while Bert was looking at a new postage stamp album he had long wanted when from the kitchen where Dinah was getting breakfast came a series of excited cries, mingled with laughter and shouts of:

"Fire! Fire! Fire!"

"Mercy! What's that?" screamed Mrs. Bobbsey, turning pale.

Mr. Bobbsey made a rush for the kitchen. Nan and Bert, with Flossie, gathered about their mother. Then they heard Dinah calling:

"Stop it, Freddie! Stop it, I tell you! Does you want me to get soaked? And you will sure spoil the pancakes!"

Mrs. Bobbsey looked relieved.

"Freddie must be up to some prank," she said.

"Freddie, stop it!" commanded Mr. Bobbsey, and then he was heard to laugh. The others all went out to the kitchen and there they saw a curious sight.

Freddie, with his new toy fire engine, was pumping water on Dinah, who was laughing so heartily that she could do nothing to stop him. Mr. Bobbsey, too, was shouting with mirth, for the hose from the toy engine was rather small and threw only a thin, fine spray.

"I'm a fireman!" cried Freddie, "and I'm pretending Dinah is on fire. See her red apron—that's the fire!" and the little fellow turned the crank of his engine harder than ever, throwing the tiny stream of water all over the kitchen.

"That's enough, Freddie," said Mr. Bobbsey,

when he could stop laughing. Dinah was still shaking with mirth, and Freddie, looking in the tank of the engine, said, "There's only a little more water left. Can't I squirt that?"

Without waiting for permission Freddie made the water spurt from the nozzle of the hose. At that moment the door of the kitchen opened, to let in Sam. With him came Snap, the trick dog, and the tiny stream of water caught Sam full in the face.

"Hello!" he said in surprise. "Is the house leaking?"

"It's my new fire engine!" cried Freddie. "I didn't mean to wet you, Sam, but I was playing Dinah was on fire!"

"Well, you didn't wet me so very much," replied Sam, with a grin. "That sure is a fine fire engine!"

Snap sprang about barking and wagging his tail, and, there being no more water in Freddie's engine, he had to stop pumping, for which everyone was glad.

"You must not do that again," said Mrs. Bobbsey, when the excitement was over. "You frightened us all, Freddie, and that is not nice, you know."

"I won't, mamma, but I did want to try my fire engine."

"Then you must do it in the bathroom where the water will do no harm. But come now, children, get your breakfast and then you will have the whole day to look at your toys."

Breakfast was rather a hurried affair, and every now and then Flossie and Freddie would leave the table to see some of their gifts. But finally the meal was over and then came more joyous times. Sam received his presents, and Mr. and Mrs. Bobbsey had time to look at theirs, for Santa Claus had not forgotten them.

"And there's something for Snap, and for Snoop too!" exclaimed Freddie. "Snoop has a new ribbon with a silver bell, and Snap a new collar with his name on it," and soon the cat and dog, newly adorned, were being put through some of their tricks.

If I tried to tell you all that went on in the Bobbsey house that Christmas this book would contain nothing else. So I will only say that the holiday was one of the most delightful the twins ever remembered.

"And then to think, with all this, that we are to go to Snow Lodge! It's great!" cried Bert.

"I hope I can get some good pictures up there with my camera," said Nan. "Will you show me how it works, Bert?"

"Yes, and we'll go out today and try it. I want to see how my new skates go, too. The lake is frozen and we'll have some fun."

The day was cold and clear. There had been a little fall of snow during the night, but not enough to spoil the skating, and soon Bert and Nan were on their way to the lake, while Flossie and Freddie, after inspecting all their presents over again, had gone out to play on their sleds.

This gave Dinah and Mrs. Bobbsey time to get ready the roast turkey for the big Christmas dinner. Mr. Bobbsey had brought home one of the largest he could find.

While Flossie and Freddie were playing on the hill, a small one near their home, they heard a voice calling to them: "Want a ride, youngsters?"

Looking up they saw Mr. Carford in his big sled. It was filled with baskets and packages, and the Bobbsey twins guessed rightly that the generous old man was taking around his Christmas contributions to the poor families.

"Yes, we'll go!" cried Freddie.

"What shall we do with our sleds?" asked Flossie.

"Oh, Harry Stone will look after them, won't you Harry?" asked Freddie. "He can use mine, and his sister Jessie can use yours until we come back, Flossie," and Freddie turned the coasters over to a poor boy and girl who lived near the Bobbsey home. Harry and his sister were delighted, and promised to take good care of the sleds.

"I won't take you far—only just around town," said Mr. Carford, as the twins got in his sled. "When are you going up to my Snow Lodge?"

"We're going soon, I guess," answered Flossie. "I heard mamma and papa talking about it yesterday."

"And we're ever so much obliged to you for letting us have your place," said Flossie. "Will you come up and see us while we're there? I've got a doll that can talk."

"And I'm going to take my fire engine along, so if the place gets on fire I can help put it out," exclaimed Freddie. "Will you come up?"

Mr. Carford started. He looked at the children in a strange sort of way, and then stared at the horses.

"No—no—I guess I won't go to Snow Lodge anymore," he said slowly, and Flossie and Freddie were sorry they had asked him, for they remembered the story their father had told them about the sorrow that had come to the aged man.

But the children soon forgot this in the joy of helping in the distribution of the good things in the sled, and the happiness brought to many poor families seemed to make up, in a way, for what Mr. Carford had suffered in the trouble over his nephew.

When all the gifts had been given out from the sled, Mr. Carford drove the two younger Bobbsey twins back to the hill where they again had fun coasting.

Meanwhile Nan and Bert were having a good time on the ice. Nan's camera was used to take a number of pictures, which the children hoped would turn out well.

While Bert was taking a picture of Nan, Charley Mason came skating up, and Bert, whose best chum he was, insisted that Charley get in the picture also.

"My!" exclaimed Charley, as he saw Nan's camera, "that's a fine one!"

"I just got it today," said Nan, with a pleased smile. "I'm going to take a lot of pictures up at Snow Lodge."

"Snow Lodge," repeated Charley. "You mean that place Mr. Carford owns?"

"Yes," replied Bert. "He is going to let us all go up there for three weeks or so."

"Say, that's funny," spoke Charley. "You'll have some other Lakeport folks near you."

"Who else is going up to Snow Lodge?" asked Nan.

"Well, they're not exactly going to Snow Lodge," replied Charley, "but I heard a while ago that Danny Rugg and his folks were going up to a winter camp near there. Mr. Rugg has bought a lumber tract in the woods, and he's going to see about having some of the trees cut. Danny is going, too. So you'll have him for a neighbor."

"Oh, dear!" exclaimed Nan, in dismay. "That spoils everything!"

"Well, if Danny tries any of his tricks I'll get after him!" exclaimed Bert, firmly. But he looked anxious over the unwelcome news Charley had brought.

CHAPTER 11

MAKING PLANS

"ARE you sure this is so—is Danny Rugg really going up to the woods near Snow Lodge?" asked Bert of Charley, after a pause.

"That's what Frank Smith told me," replied Charley, "and you know Frank and Danny are great chums."

"That's so. Well, if Danny doesn't bother us we won't make any trouble for him," said Bert. "Still, I'd rather he would go somewhere else."

"If Mr. Rugg is going up to see about having lumber cut," said Nan, "I guess there won't be much fun for Danny. Maybe he won't bother us at all."

"He will if he gets a chance," declared her brother. "Danny's just that kind. But we'll wait and see."

Bert, Nan, and Charley talked for some time longer about the trip to Snow Lodge, and then, as it was getting nearly time for dinner, they skated down the lake toward their homes.

"How are you folks going up to the lodge?" asked Charley, before parting from Bert and Nan.

"Oh, I guess father will take one of his big lumber sleds and drive us all up," replied Bert. "We'll have to take along lots of things to eat, for it's a good ways to the store, and we might get snowed in."

"That's right," said Charley. "But say, why don't you and Freddie go up in our ice boat, the *Ice Bird*? It isn't much of a run to Snow Lodge on the lake, and it's good going now."

"I never thought of that!" exclaimed Bert. "I wonder if father would let us?"

"You can ask him," said Nan. "I'd like to skate up, if it wasn't so far. But I don't believe it would be safe to take Freddie on the ice boat, Bert. He's so little, and so easily excited that he might tumble out."

"That's right. And yet it will be no fun to sail it alone. I wish you could go with me, Charley."

"I wish I could, but I don't see how I can. My folks are going to my grandmother's for a couple of weeks. Otherwise I'd be glad to go."

"Well, maybe my father will sail in the ice boat with me," spoke Bert. "I guess I'll ask him."

Bert and Nan had much to talk about as they skated on, having bidden Charley good-bye, and their conversation was mostly about the new idea of getting to Snow Lodge on the ice.

"I don't want to skate alone, any more than you want to go in the ice boat alone," said Nan. "But maybe mamma and papa will let us invite some of our friends to spend a week or so at Snow Lodge with us. Then it would be all right."

"It surely would," said Bert.

The Christmas dinner at the Bobbsey home was a jolly affair, and while it was being eaten Bert spoke to his father about the ice boat.

"Do you think it will carry you to the upper end of the lake?" asked Mr. Bobbsey with a smile, for Bert and Charley had made the boat themselves, with a little help. Though it was a homemade affair, Bert was as proud of it as though a large sum had been spent for it.

"Of course it will carry us to Snow Lodge," he said. "There would be room for four or five on it, if the wind was strong enough to carry us to the head of the lake. But I don't want to go alone, father. Could you come?"

"I'm afraid not," laughed Mr. Bobbsey. "I'll have to go in the big sled with your mother, and the provisions. We're going to take Dinah and Sam along, you know. Can't you ask some of your friends? I guess there's room enough at the Lodge."

"That's just what I'll do!" exclaimed Bert. "I'll

see who of the boys can go."

"And may I ask Grace Lavine or Nellie Parks?" inquired Nan. "We could skate up or go part of the way in the ice boat with the boys."

"I think so," said Mrs. Bobbsey.

After a while the plum pudding was served. Freddie begged that Snoop and Snap be given an extra good dinner, on account of it being Christmas, and Dinah promised to see to this.

Mr. and Mrs. Bobbsey discussed the plans for going to Snow Lodge. They agreed that Bert and Nan, if they wished, might each ask a friend, for the old farmhouse in the woods on the edge of the lake contained many rooms. It was completely furnished, all that was needed being food.

"So if you young folks want to skate or take the ice boat up the lake I see no objection," said Mr. Bobbsey. "The rest of us will go in a big sled."

"Couldn't I go in the ice boat?" asked Freddie. "I'm getting big. I'm almost in the first reader book."

"We're going so fast your fire engine might be lost overboard," said Bert with a smile, and that was enough for his little brother. He didn't want that to happen for the world, so he gave up the plan of going on the *Ice Bird*.

"I don't like the idea of that Danny Rugg going to be near us," said Mrs. Bobbsey to her husband, when Bert had told this news. "He's sure to make trouble."

"Perhaps not," said Mr. Bobbsey. "Bert generally manages to hold his own when Danny bothers him."

"Yes, I know. But it always makes hard feelings. I do wish Danny wasn't going up there."

"Well, the woods are open, and we can't stop him," said Mr. Bobbsey, with a smile. The children had gone out to play, and the house was quiet once more.

"There is a great deal to do to get ready," went on Mrs. Bobbsey. "But I think the trip will do us all good. I only hope none of us take cold."

"Don't worry," advised her husband. "I'll see Mr. Carford, and have the fires made up a couple of days before we arrive. That will make the house good and warm, and dry it out."

They talked over the various things they had to do in order to make their stay at Snow Lodge pleasant, and then went out to call on some friends.

That afternoon Bert and Nan extended the invitation to Snow Lodge to a number of their boy and girl friends, explaining how they were going to make the trip on skates or on the ice boat.

But one after another declined. Either their parents had made other plans for spending the Christmas holidays, or they did not think it wise to let their children go off in the woods.

Bert asked a number of boys he knew, but none of them could go, and Grace Lavine, Nellie Parks, and many other girls to whom Nan spoke, made excuses.

"I guess we'll have to give up the ice boat plan," said Bert regretfully that night to Nan. "No one seems able to go. Will you risk it with me, Nan?"

"I wouldn't be afraid," she answered. "If mamma and papa will let me I'll sail in the *Ice Bird* with you."

"Then we'll go that way!" cried Bert. But the next day something occurred that made a change in the plans of the Bobbsey twins.

CHAPTER 12

THE LETTERS

THE day after Christmas, when Bert and Nan came home from having been to see a number of their friends but had not succeeded in getting any of them to promise to make the trip to Snow Lodge, the two older Bobbsey twins were quite discouraged.

"I'll need another fellow to help me sail the ice boat," spoke Bert. "Of course I know you'll do all you can, Nan, but we can't tell what might happen. I don't see what's the matter with all the fellows, anyhow, that they can't go."

"And the girls, too," added Nan. "I couldn't get one of them to promise. And I don't know whether mamma and papa will let you and me go in the ice boat by ourselves."

And, when they heard of this plan, both Mr. and Mrs. Bobbsey objected to it.

"It would be too risky," decided Mr. Bobbsey. "Your ice boat is a small one, I know, Bert, but in a stiff wind it might capsize if you did not have some other boy along to help you manage it. I guess you and Nan had better come with us in the big sled."

"I think so, too," added Mrs. Bobbsey.

There seemed to be no other way out of it, and Nan and Bert felt quite badly. Not even the tricks of Snap and Snoop, when Freddie and Flossie put the dog and cat through them before going to bed, would cause their older brother and sister to look happy.

"Never mind," said Mamma Bobbsey, "when we get to Snow Lodge you'll have such a good time that you won't mind not having made the trip on skates or on the ice boat. And you can skate all you like when you get up there."

The next day Freddie was playing quite a game. He had a little toy village, made of pasteboard houses, and this he had set up in the playroom. He was pretending that a fire had broken out in one of the dwellings and he was going to put it out with his toy engine. Of course there was not even a match on fire, for Mrs. Bobbsey was very careful about this, but Freddie pretended to his heart's content. He was allowed to have real water, but Dinah had spread on the floor an old rubber coat so that the spray would do no harm.

With a great shout Freddie came running out of the "engine house," which was a chair turned on its side. He was pulling his toy after him, racing to the make-believe blaze.

Just then Flossie came into the room with her new walking doll, and, not seeing her, Freddie ran into her and knocked her over.

Flossie sat down quite hard, and for a moment was too surprised to cry. But a moment later, when she saw Freddie's fire engine run over her new doll, which cried out "mamma!" as if in pain, the tears came into Flossie's eyes.

"Oh, you bad boy!" she exclaimed, forgetting her own pain at the sight of her doll, "you've run right over her!"

"I–I couldn't help it!" said Freddie, stopping in his rush to the fire to pick up his sister's toy. "You got right in my way."

"I did not–Freddie Bobbsey."

"Yes you did, too, and I'm going to squirt water on you and put you out. You're on fire! Your cheeks are all red!"

This was true enough. Flossie did get very red cheeks when she was excited.

"Don't you put any water on me!" she cried. "I'll tell mamma on you! And you've broke my best doll, too! Oh, dear!" and Flossie burst into tears so there was no need for Freddie to use his toy engine to wet her flaming cheeks.

This frightened Freddie. He seldom made his

twin sister cry, and he was very much alarmed.

"I–I didn't mean to, Flossie," he said, putting his arms around her. "I guess I was running pretty fast. Don't cry, and you can squirt my engine. Maybe if you squirted some water on your doll she'd be all right," and Freddie picked up the talking toy.

"Don't you dare put any water on her!" screamed Flossie. "You'll make her catch cold, and then she won't talk at all. Oh, dear! I wish you didn't have that old engine."

It was good that Mrs. Bobbsey came into the room just then, or there is no telling what might have happened. She knew what to do, and soon she had straightened out matters. It was not very often that Flossie and Freddie had trouble of this kind, but they were only human children, just like any others, and they had their little disputes now and then.

"Oh, dear! This will never do!" said Mrs. Bobbsey. "Freddie, you must not rush about the house so fast."

"But, mamma, firemens is always fast. They have to be fast, and I was going to a fire," the fat little fellow said.

"I know, dear, but you should look where you are going. And, Flossie, dear, you must watch out before you rush into a room, you know."

"Yes, mamma, but I was pretending my doll was sick, and I was running to the doctor's with her."

"Oh, dear!" cried Mrs. Bobbsey. "You were both in too much of a hurry, I think. Never mind. Let's see if the doll is hurt much."

It seemed that she was, for though she would walk across the room when wound up, she would not cry out "mamma!" But Mrs. Bobbsey was used to mending broken toys and after poking about in the wheels and springs with a hairpin she soon had the doll so it would talk again. Then Flossie was happy, and her tears were forgotten.

Freddie said he was sorry he had been in such a hurry, so all was forgiven, and he went on playing fireman. He was in the midst of putting out a make-believe blaze in the village church when the door-bell rang and the postman's whistle was heard.

"Will you get the mail, dear?" asked Mrs. Bobbsey of Freddie. "Dinah is busy, I'm sure. Let me see how mamma's little Fat Fireman can get the letters. But don't run!" she exclaimed, "or you might fall downstairs."

"I won't, mamma," said Freddie.

He came back with several letters and he was again playing he was a fireman, and Flossie was making believe she was a doctor for her sick dolls when Mrs. Bobbsey exclaimed: "Oh, this will be good news for Bert," and she looked up from a letter she was reading.

"What is it, mamma?" asked Flossie. "Is someone sending him more Christmas presents?"

"No, dear, but Harry, your cousin from the country, is coming to visit us. Bert will have someone to play with. Won't that be nice?"

"And can I play with him, too?" asked Freddie.

"I guess so, sometimes," said Mrs. Bobbsey. "But you must remember that Harry is about ten years old, and he won't always want to be with little boys."

"I'm a big boy!" declared Freddie. "I'm 'most as big as Bert."

"Well, I guess you can have some fun," said Mrs. Bobbsey. "Bert will be glad to hear this. Now, who can this other letter be from?" and she tore open the envelope.

"Why!" she cried, as she quickly read it. "It's from Uncle William Minturn at the seashore, and he says his daughter Dorothy is coming to pay us a visit. Well, did you ever! Our two cousins—one from the country and the other from the seashore—both coming at the same time! Oh, this will please Bert and Nan!"

"And can't we have a good time, too?" asked Flossie.

"Of course," said Mrs. Bobbsey. "Let me see now; how will I arrange the rooms for them? Oh, I forgot, we're going to Snow Lodge soon. I wonder what I can do? Both Dorothy and Harry will be here before I can tell them not to come. I must telephone to papa!"

Bert and Nan came in just then in time to hear this last sentence.

"Telephone to papa!" exclaimed Bert. "What's the matter, mother? Has anything happened?"

"Nothing, only your cousins, Dorothy and Harry, are coming to visit you. And I don't know what to do about it as we are going to Snow Lodge!"

"Do about it?" cried Bert. "Why, we won't do anything about it, except to let them come. Say, this is the best news yet! Harry can go with me on the ice boat. Hurray! Hurray!"

"Yes, and Dorothy and I can skate on the lake!" said Nan. "Oh, how glad I am!"

"We'll take them both to Snow Lodge!" cried Bert. "Now we won't have to look for any other boys or girls. We'll have our own cousins! Whoop!" and he threw his arms around his mother, while Nan tried to kiss her. Flossie and Freddie looked on in pleased surprise. The letters had come just in time. Now there would be a jolly part at Snow Lodge.

CHAPTER 13

IN A HARD BLOW

"ARE you girls warm enough?" asked Bert Bobbsey, as he and his cousin Harry started toward the frozen lake one afternoon, the day before they were all to start for Snow Lodge.

"If we aren't we will never be," answered Dorothy Minturn, who was Nan's "seashore cousin." "I've got on so many things that it would be easier to roll along instead of walking," went on Dorothy with a laugh.

"Well, it's a good thing to be warm, for it will be cold on the ice boat, won't it, Bert?" asked Harry.

"That's what it will. There's a good wind blowing, too. It's stronger than I thought it was," and Bert bent to the blast as he walked along with the others.

"Will there be any danger?" asked Dorothy, who was not used to the activities of the Bobbseys.

"Oh, don't worry!" cried Harry. "We'll look after you girls."

"They think they will," murmured Nan, looking at her cousin. "I guess I know almost as much about the *Ice Bird* as Bert does."

"Where is your ice boat?" asked Harry of Bert, as they kept on along the path that led to the lake.

"Over in the next cove. I had her out the other day and the wind died out, leaving me there. Since then we've been so busy getting ready to go to Snow Lodge that I haven't had time to bring her back to the dock."

"Will she be safe over there?"

"I guess so—hardly anybody goes there in winter."

The two cousins—Harry from the country and Dorothy from the seashore—in each of which places the Bobbseys had spent part of the preceding summer, had followed soon after their letters, and had been warmly welcomed by Nan, Bert, Flossie, and Freddie. The visitors were rather surprised to learn that the Bobbsey family was preparing to go away for a winter vacation in the woods, but they were only too glad to accept an invitation to go along.

So it was arranged, and in another day the start to Mr. Carford's former home would be made. Mr. Bobbsey had gotten a big sled ready with boxes, barrels, and packages of provisions. Snow Lodge had been opened by a farmer living near there, who remained in it all night, keeping up the fires so that the long-deserted house would not be chilly, and all was in readiness.

The plans of Nan and Bert to go to Snow Lodge by means of skates and on the ice boat had been agreed to.

Dorothy and Nan thought they would rather skate than go all the way on the ice boat, but Bert and Harry decided to keep to the ice craft all the way.

"And when you girls get tired of skating just wave your handkerchiefs, and we'll wait for you," said Bert.

Now they were going to take a little trial sail on the *Ice Bird* before starting off on the longer cruise.

As the four walked around a point of land, and came within sight of the ice boat, tied to a stake in the ice of the cove, Harry uttered a cry.

"Look!" he exclaimed to Bert, "someone is at your boat!"

"That's right!" cried Bert, starting to run. Just then a figure skated away from the craft, and Bert breathed a sigh of relief.

"I guess it was only someone taking a look at her," he said. "There aren't many on the lake."

"We can't go very far," said Nan, as they neared the boat, "for mamma said to be back early. We've got a great deal of packing to do yet."

"We'll just take a little spin," replied Bert.

They were soon on the ice boat, gliding up and

down the lake, which was frozen to a glassy smoothness.

"If it's like this tomorrow it will be grand for skating!" exclaimed Nan.

"Yes, and fine for ice-boating, too," replied her brother. "We'll beat you to Snow Lodge."

"Well, you ought to," said Dorothy, "but we'll be warmer skating than you will be on the ice boat."

"Not when we take along all the fur robes I've got out for the trip," replied Bert. "I didn't bring 'em this time, as it was too far to carry. But tomorrow Harry and I will be regular Eskimos."

Back and forth on the lake sailed the *Ice Bird* with the merry-hearted boys and girls. Bert did not go very far, as he noticed that the wind was growing much stronger and his boat, though sturdy and well-built, was not intended to weather a gale.

"Well, I think we'd better start for home now," said Nan after about an hour's sailing. "Mamma will be expecting us."

"All right," assented Bert. "Do you want to steer her, Harry?"

"I'm afraid I don't know how," replied the country lad.

"Oh, you'll soon learn. I'll be right beside you here, and tell you what to do."

"Don't upset, please, whatever you do," urged Dorothy.

"I'll try not to," promised Harry.

When they got out of the sheltered cover, they felt the full force of the wind, and for a moment even Nan, who had been on the boat many times, felt a bit timid. The *Ice Bird* tilted to one side, the left-hand runner raising high in the air.

"Oh!" screamed Dorothy. "We're going over."

"No, we're not! Sit still!" cried Bert, grasping the tiller, which Harry was not holding just right. By turning the ice boat to one side the wind did not strike it so hard, and the craft settled down on the level again.

"There! That's better!" exclaimed Dorothy, who had grabbed hold of Nan.

"Oh, that's nothing," said Nan. "Bert and I are used to that."

But as the ice boat proceeded it was evident that those on her were not going to have an easy time to get to the Bobbsey dock. The wind blew harder and harder, and the sail seemed ready to rip apart. It took both Bert and Harry to hold the rudder steady, and even then the tiller was almost torn from their grasp.

Even Nan began to look a little frightened, and she did not laugh when Dorothy stretched out flat and held on to the side of the boat with all her strength.

"I don't want to be blown away if I can help it," said Dorothy.

Harder and harder blew the wind, sending the ice boat along at great speed. In a few minutes more it would be at the dock where Bert kept it tied.

"If it blows this way tomorrow we won't be long getting to Snow Lodge," cried Bert in Harry's ear. He had to shout to be heard above the howling of the wind.

"That's right," agreed the country boy. "The girls can never skate along as fast as this."

"We'll have to use less sail," went on Bert, "and then we won't go so fast."

He and Harry shifted the rudder to steer closer to shore. Suddenly the wind came in a fierce gust. The ice boat seemed about to turn completely over. The two girls screamed, even Nan being frightened now.

"Oh, what is it? What is it?" cried Dorothy.

Then came a sharp crack. There was a sound as though a hundred popguns were being fired, and the boat slackened speed.

"Look!" cried Harry, pointing ahead. "Our sail has burst, Bert."

"No, it's the sheet rope—the main rope that holds the sail fast—that's broken," replied Bert. "Lucky it did, too, or we might have gone over. I was going to let go of it."

The ice boat slid along a short distance, and

then came to a stop. The sail, no longer held in place so as to catch the wind, was blowing and flapping, making snapping sounds like a line of clothes in a heavy wind.

"All right, girls, no danger now," called Bert, as he got out to make the flapping sail fast again. As he looked at the end of the broken rope he uttered a cry of surprise.

"Look here!" he called to Harry, "this rope has been cut!"

"Cut?"

"Yes. Someone hacked it partly through with a knife, and the wind did the rest."

There was no doubt of it. The main rope had been partly severed, and the strain of the hard blow had done the rest.

"That fellow we saw near the ice boat!" began Harry. "It must have been him! Who was he?"

"Danny Rugg–if anybody," answered Bert. "I thought it looked like him. Probably he heard that we were going to use the boat to go to Snow Lodge, and he wanted to make trouble for us. He's going to camp up there near us, I hear."

"Gracious!" cried Dorothy. "I hope he doesn't play any tricks like that up there."

"If he does I guess Harry and I can attend to him," cried Bert. "But, in a way, it's a good thing the rope did break or we might have upset. Only

Danny, if he did it, had no idea of doing us a good turn. He just wanted to make trouble."

"Can you fix it?" asked Nan of her brother.

"Oh, yes, it can be spliced and will be stronger than ever. But I won't do it now. We can walk the rest of the way to the dock. The wind is blowing harder than ever, and we don't want any accidents."

Indeed, the wind was blowing a gale now, and even with the sail down the ice boat went along at such a speed that it was all Harry and Bert could do to hold it.

But finally it was gotten to the dock and made fast, and while the girls went on to the Bobbsey home to finish with their packing, Bert and Harry mended the broken rope.

"I'll have to teach Danny Rugg a good lesson," said Bert to his cousin.

"Yes, and I'll help you," returned Harry.

CHAPTER 14

AT SNOW LODGE

"ARE we all here?"

"Have we got everything?"

"Here, Snap! If you jump out again you can't go!"

"Dinah, you hold Snap, will you?"

"How can I? I've got about all I can do to hold my own self!"

These were some of the cries and exclamations as the Bobbsey family prepared to start on the trip to Snow Lodge. With the exception of Nan and Bert, and Dorothy and Harry, they were all in a big sled, drawn by four horses that were prancing about in the snow, anxious to get started. At every step the bells jingled. Sam was driving, and with him on the front seat sat fat Freddie.

"I'm going to drive as soon as we get out on the country road!" cried Freddie.

"He is not, is he, Sam?" demanded Flossie, who was taking one of her dolls on the trip, and with the doll and her big muff little Flossie had about all she could manage.

"Yes, I am too," declared Freddie. "You said I could, Sam, you know you did!"

"Well I guess you can drive where the roads are easy," promised the handyman.

Mr. and Mrs. Bobbsey were now on their seat, with Flossie between them. Dinah was on the seat behind, while in back of her were piled the packages of food.

Snap, the trick dog, was to be taken along, but it had been decided to leave Downy the duck, and Snoop the fat black cat, at home. A neighbor had promised to look after them and feed them.

"Well, I guess we're all ready," said Mr. Bobbsey, as he looked back at the well-loaded sled. "Now be careful," he called to Nan and Bert, who with their cousins were to go to Snow Lodge on the icy lake. The girls would skate part of the way and ride on the ice boat the remainder of the distance.

"We'll be careful," said Bert.

The day was cold, and clouds overhead seemed to tell that it was going to snow. But the young folks hoped the storm would hold off until night, when they would be safe in the big, old-fashioned farmhouse.

Everyone was well wrapped up, and Flossie and

Freddie were almost lost in big rugs that had been tucked around them, for their mother did not want them to get cold.

Piles of rugs and blankets had been put on the ice boat so those aboard would be comfortable.

"Well, let's start!" called Mr. Bobbsey finally. "We'll see who will get there first, Bert or us."

"All right—a race then!" cried Nan.

Down to the glittering icy lake went the boys and girls, down to where the ice boat awaited them. It had been put in good shape for the trip, but before starting Bert and Harry looked over all the ropes to make sure none were frayed, or had been cut. Nothing had been seen of Danny Rugg, and Charley Mason told Bert he thought the bully had gone to the wood camp with his father.

"Don't you girls want to come on the ice boat for a ways first?" asked Bert of his sister and Dorothy. "Then, when you get tired of riding, you can skate."

"Shall we?" inquired Nan.

"I guess so," answered Dorothy, and so they did. The wind was not as strong as it had been the day before, but it was enough of a breeze to send the *Ice Bird* along at a good speed. Well wrapped in the robes and blankets, the young people enjoyed the trip very much.

"I'm sure we'll be there before papa and mamma are," said Nan as they glided along. "See how fast we are going."

"Yes, but this wind may not keep up all the way," spoke her brother. "And it's a good way to Snow Lodge."

"Oh well, we'll have a good time, anyhow," said Dorothy.

"And we'll stop and build a fire and have lunch when we're hungry," added Harry, for they had brought some food with them, and could make chocolate over a little fire.

Meanwhile the sled-load of the other Bobbseys, Sam and Dinah, and Snap, was proceeding along the snowy road. The path had been well broken, and the going was good, so they made fairly fast time. But every now and then Snap would insist on jumping out to run along the road, and every time he did this Flossie and Freddie would set up a howl, fearing he would get lost.

"Snap!" exclaimed Mr. Bobbsey, when this had happened four or five times, "if you don't stay here quietly I'll tie you fast. Lie down, sir!"

Snap barked, wagged his tail, and looked at Mr. Bobbsey with his head tilted to one side as much as to say, "Very well, sir. I'll be good now. But I did want a little run." Then Snap curled up at Dinah's feet and gave no more trouble.

"I say," exclaimed the cook, with a laugh that made her shake all over. "Snap is a good foot-warmer. I just hope he doesn't jump out anymore." And, for a time at least, the trick dog seemed content to lie quietly in the sled.

It was not a very exciting trip for those in the sled, as they went along through the streets of Lakeport and so out into the open country. Then they passed through village after village, with little occurring. The roads were good, and occasionally they met other teams.

Once they came to a narrow place between two big drifts, and as another sled was coming toward them it was rather a race to see which one would get to the opening first.

"You can't go through when he does, Sam," said Mr. Bobbsey, nodding toward the other driver.

"I know I can't, sir. But I'll get there first."

Sam called to his horses and they sprang forward. A little later they had reached the opening between the drifts, and the other sled had to wait until the Bobbseys got out of the narrow place.

All this time Bert and the others were making their way up the lake on the ice. After going a mile or two on the ice boat the wind died down so that the craft did not go very fast.

"Come on, Dorothy," called Nan, "let's skate for a while. And if you get too far ahead of us, please wait, Bert," she added, and her brother promised that he and Harry would.

For a time Dorothy and Nan enjoyed the skating very much, and it was a welcome change from sitting still on the ice boat. Then the wind sprang up again, and Harry and Bert got so far ahead that the two girls thought they should never be able to skate to them.

"Oh, I wish they'd wait," said Dorothy. "I'm getting tired."

"I'll wave to them—maybe they'll see my handkerchief," said Nan.

Bert and Harry did see the girls, and, guessing what the white signal meant, they lowered the sail of the ice boat and waited for the two to come up. And the girls were glad enough now to sit amid the comfortable robes and blankets.

"Skating such a long distance is harder than I thought it would be," confessed Nan, with a sigh.

"Yes, the ice boat is good enough for me," agreed Dorothy. "But when we get to Snow Lodge we'll do some skating."

"That's what we will," said Nan.

Mile after mile was covered by the *Ice Bird.* They passed small towns and villages on the shore of the frozen lake. Many of the places were known to Nan and Bert, who had often visited them in the summertime, rowing to them in their boat, or sailing to them with the older folks.

"Isn't it almost time to eat?" asked Bert, after a bit. "That sun looks as if it were noon, Nan."

"It's half-past eleven," spoke Harry, glancing at his watch. "There's a nice little cove where we can be out of the wind, and where we can build a fire," he went on, pointing ahead.

"That's what we'll do!" cried Bert, steering toward it. "Now you girls will have a chance to show what sort of cooks you are."

"Humph! There's nothing to cook but chocolate!" said Nan. "Anyone could make that."

They had brought with them the chocolate all ready to heat in a pot, and soon it was set over a fire of sticks that the boys had made on shore, scraping away the snow from the ground. Nan and Dorothy got out the packages of sandwiches and cake, and soon a merry little party was seated on the ice boat, eating the good things.

The meal was soon over and then the young people got ready to resume their trip. Nan and Dorothy wanted to skate a bit, but Bert, looking up at the sky, said, "I don't think it will be safe. It looks as though it is going to storm soon, and we don't want to be caught in it. It isn't far to Snow Lodge now, and once we are there, let it snow as much as it likes. But if it comes down before we get there we'll have hard work to keep on in the ice boat. Even a little snow on the ice will clog the runners."

So the skating idea was given up, and soon they were underway in the ice boat again. The clouds grew darker, and there were a few scattering flakes of snow.

"I guess we're going to be in for it," said Bert. "If the wind would only blow harder we could go faster."

As if in answer to his wish the wind started up and the boat fairly flew over the ice. Then the storm suddenly broke and the snow was so thick that they could not see where they were going.

"What shall we do?" cried Dorothy, who was not used to being out in such a blow.

"Keep on–that's the only thing to do," answered Bert. "We will go as far as we can in the boat and then we'll walk."

"Walk to Snow Lodge!" cried Nan. "We could never do it!"

"Oh, it isn't so far now," said her brother.

The snow fell so fast that soon the ice boat went slower and slower. Finally it stopped altogether, the runners clogged with snow. The wind blowing on the sail nearly turned the craft over.

"Cast off those ropes!" cried Bert to Harry. "We'll have to leave her here and walk on."

The sail was lowered, the blankets and robes

were picked up to be carried, and the four girls and boys set out over the ice.

"We must keep near the shore," said Bert. "Snow Lodge is right on the shore of the lake, and we can't miss it."

"Oh, suppose we did, and had to stay out all night?" cried Dorothy.

"We won't worry until we have to," spoke Nan.

It snowed harder and harder, and grew quite dark. Even Bert was worried. He and Harry walked on ahead, to keep the wind and snow as much as possible out of the faces of the girls.

"Bert, I'm sure we're lost!" cried Nan a little later. "We can't see where we're going! Don't go on any further."

"We can't stay here on the ice all night," objected Bert.

"Well, it is pretty dark," said Harry. "Are there are any houses around here?"

They gazed at the fast-gathering blackness all around them. They were beginning to be very much afraid. The wind howled, and the snow came down harder than ever.

"There's a light!" suddenly called Dorothy.

"Where?" cried all the others eagerly.

"There," answered Dorothy, pointing toward where they had last seen the land. "Right over there in those trees."

"Then let's go toward it," suggested Bert. "Maybe they can tell us where Snow Lodge is, and if it's too far we'll stay there all night if they'll let us."

The welcome light shone out through the storm and darkness. The four young folks made their way toward it as best they could, and, as they came nearer they could see that it was a big house in the midst of trees. Bert rubbed his eyes. He looked again, and then he cried, "Why, it's Snow Lodge! It's Snow Lodge! We've found it after all! We're all right now! We're at Snow Lodge!"

"Hurray!" cried Harry.

"Oh, how glad I am!" said Nan, with her arms around Dorothy.

A door opened and the light streamed out over the snow.

"Who is there?" called Mr. Bobbsey. "Is that you, Bert?"

"Yes, father. We're here at last."

"Oh, thank goodness!" said Mrs. Bobbsey. "We were just going out to search for you!"

CHAPTER 15

THE SNOWSLIDE

How warm and cozy it was in Snow Lodge! How bright were the lights, and how the big fire blazed, crackled, and roared up the chimney! And what a delightful smell came from the kitchen! It could easily be told that Dinah was out there.

"Where you have been?"

"What happened to you?"

"Was there an accident?"

"Did you get lost?"

"Did the ice boat sink?"

It was Freddie and Flossie who asked the last two questions, and Mr. and Mrs. Bobbsey who asked the others as Bert, Nan, Harry, and Dorothy came into the farmhouse. Oh, how good it seemed after their battle in the darkness with the storm!

"The ice boat couldn't go on account of the snow," explained Bert, "so we had to leave it and walk."

"And we got lost," added Nan. "Oh, it was terrible out there on the frozen lake!"

"Indeed it was," agreed Dorothy. "I never had such a time in all my life."

"It was too bad," said Mrs. Bobbsey. "You children should have come in the sled with us."

"Oh, we didn't mind it much," spoke Harry. "We had a good lunch. We saw the light and thought it was some farmhouse. We didn't think it was Snow Lodge. But we're glad it is," he added with a laugh.

"We got here some time ago," said Mr. Bobbsey. "The farmer had the fires all going finely, and it was as warm as toast. We began getting things to rights, but when it got dark and snowed and you children weren't here, we all got worried."

"And we were going to look for you," added Mrs. Bobbsey. "Oh, I was so worried I didn't know what to do!"

The evening was spent in playing a few games, and in talking and telling stories. Everyone was too tired to stay up long, after the day's trip, and so "early to bed" was the rule, for the first night at least.

As Bert went up to his room with his cousin Harry he looked out of the window. It was too dark to see much, but the boy could get a glimpse of the snow blowing against the panes with great force.

"Poor Henry Burdock!" thought Bert. "If it

wasn't for that missing money he and his uncle might be living here at Snow Lodge. I wonder where Harry is now? Maybe off somewhere in the woods, lost—as we nearly were!"

The thought made him feel sad. Surely it was a terrible night to be out in the forest, amid the storm and darkness.

"I wish I could help him," thought Bert, but he did not see how he could. Mr. Carford was a stern old man, and he believed that his nephew had taken the money that was missing.

The storm raged all night, and part of the next day. Then it cleared off, leaving a great coating of white in the woods and over the fields.

"No skating or ice-boating now," said Bert, "and not for some days. We'll have to wait for a thaw and another freeze."

"But we can take walks in the woods, can't we?" asked Nan. "Would you like that, Dorothy?"

"Indeed I would," was the answer.

"Can't we come?" asked Freddie. "Flossie and I have rubber boots."

"Yes, you may come for a little way," said Bert. "We won't go far. Say, Harry, we ought to have snowshoes for this sort of thing."

"That's right," agreed his cousin. "I saw a picture of some, but I don't believe I would know how to make them."

"I made some once, but they weren't much good," admitted Bert. "We'll get my father to show us how some day. It would be fun to take a trip on them over the snow."

Well wrapped up, the young folks set off through the woods, Snap trotting along with them, barking joyously. All about Snow Lodge, back from the lake and on either side, were dense woods, and under the trees the snow was not as deep as in the open fields, for the branches kept part of it off. But it was deep enough to make walking hard.

"We can't go very far at this rate," said Nan, as she and Dorothy struggled on through the drifts.

"Let's go to that hill, and see what sort of view there is," suggested Harry.

"All right," agreed Bert.

"And we can stop there and eat our lunch," put in Freddie.

"Our lunch!" exclaimed Nan. "We didn't bring any lunch, dearie!"

"Flossie and I did!" cried the little "Fat Fireman," as his papa often called Freddie. "We thought we'd get hungry, so we had Dinah make us some sandwiches, and give us a piece of cake."

"I'm hungry now," said Flossie, and from under her cloak she drew out a bundle, which she opened, showing a rather crumpled sandwich and a piece of cake.

"I'm going to eat, too," decided Freddie, as he brought out his lunch.

"Well, I declare, you two are the greatest ever!" cried Bert. "But it was a good idea all the same!"

"Yes, I could eat something myself!" admitted Harry. "I guess this air makes you hungry."

"We—we haven't got enough for all of us—I guess," said Freddie, looking wistfully at the package.

"Don't worry!" answered Harry with a laugh. "I won't take any, Freddie. I can wait until we get home."

Thereupon the two smaller twins proceeded to eat the lunch they had brought, doing this while trudging through the snow toward the little hill.

They reached the top, and stood for a time looking over the broad snow-covered expanse of lake and woods. Then they started down. But it was not easy work, especially for Flossie and Freddie, so the whole party stopped for a rest about halfway.

They were sitting under a sheltering tree looking at some flitting snowbirds when from behind them came a curious sound. Bert looked back, and leaping to his feet, cried: "It's a snowslide! A snowslide! It's coming right toward us!"

Indeed a great drift of the white snow was sliding down the side of the hill toward the children. A great white ball seemed to have started it, and as

Harry looked up he gave a cry of surprise.

"I saw a boy up there!" he said. "He pushed that snowball on us!"

CHAPTER 16

LOST IN THE WOODS

"QUICK!" cried Bert, as he looked at the swiftly sliding snow, "get close to the tree—on the downward side of it, and maybe the drift will go around us. Harry, you look after Freddie, and I'll take care of Flossie!"

As he spoke Bert grabbed up his little sister and hurried closer to the tree. It was a big pine, and they had been sitting under its branches, on some big rocks, as the slide started.

"What shall we do?" cried Nan. "Can't Dorothy and I help?"

"Take care of yourselves," answered Bert. "I guess it will split at the tree and not hurt us."

The snowslide had started at the top of the hill, whether from some snowball a boy had made and rolled down, or from some other cause, Bert did not stop to consider. He was too anxious to get his little brother and sister to safety.

The snow was rather soft, and just right for the

making of big balls of the kind that had been put on the school steps. And, as it continued to slide down the hill, the mass of snow got larger and larger until it was big enough to frighten even older persons than the Bobbsey twins and their cousins.

Harry had reached the tree with Freddie at the same time that Bert came to the protecting trunk with his little sister. Nan and Dorothy also were struggling toward it.

"Form in line!" cried Bert. "In a long string down the hill, everyone stand right in line with the tree. The big trunk may split the snowslide in two."

He and Harry took their positions nearest the trunk, with Flossie and Freddie between them. Nan and Dorothy came next. Bert clasped the tree trunk with both arms, and told Harry to grasp him as tightly as he could.

"And you and Flossie hold on to Harry, Freddie," Bert directed. "Nan, you and Dorothy hold on to the little ones. Here she comes!"

By this time the snowslide had reached the tree, and the mass was now much larger than at first. Freddie and Flossie felt like crying but they were brave and did not. It was an anxious moment.

Then just what Bert had hoped would happen came to pass. The snowslide was split in two by the tree trunk and slid to either side, leaving the Bobbsey twins and their cousins safe.

"Oh!" gasped Nan.

"What was that you said about seeing someone up there on top of the hill?" asked Bert of Harry a little later.

"I did see someone there just before the snow began to slide, and I'm almost sure I saw him roll the ball down that started the slide," answered Harry.

"Is that so? Could you see his face?"

"Not very well."

"Never mind. You don't know Danny Rugg anyhow."

"Oh, Bert! Do you think Danny could have done such a thing as that?" asked Nan in shocked tones.

"He might, not thinking how dangerous it would be," answered her brother. "I'm going up there and take a look."

"What for?" asked Dorothy.

"To see if I can find any marks in the snow. If someone was up there making a big snowball to roll down on us there will be some marks on it. And if it was Danny Rugg I'll have something to say to him."

"He wouldn't be there now, probably," said Harry. "But do you think it would be safe to go up the side of the hill?"

"Yes, it would, by keeping right in the path of

where the snowslide came down," answered Bert. "There's hardly any more snow to come down now."

"Then I'll go with you," said Harry.

Leaving the two girls and Freddie and Flossie at the tree, Bert and Harry made their way up to the top of the slope. There they saw the signs of where someone—a boy to judge by the marks of his shoes—had tramped about, rolling a big snowball.

"That's what happened," decided Bert. "Danny Rugg or some other mean chap started that slide toward us. And I think it must have been Danny. He's up around here somewhere, and he's the only one who would have a grudge against me."

Several days went by at the Lodge, and they were very busy ones. As soon as breakfast was over the boys and girls would go for a walk or would coast downhill on a slope not far away from the old farmhouse. Freddie and Flossie were not allowed to go very far away, as it was hard traveling. But they had good times around the house, and out in the old barn.

Bert and Harry made snowshoes out of barrel staves, fastening them to their feet with straps. They managed to walk fairly well on the crust.

The lake was still covered with a coating of snow and there was no skating, nor could the ice boat be used. Mr. Bobbsey, with Harry and Bert, took the team of horses one afternoon and went after the *Ice Bird.* They found it where Bert had left it the night of the storm, and hitching the horses to it, pulled the craft to the dock in front of Snow Lodge.

"It will be all ready for us when the snow is gone," said Bert.

The nights in Snow Lodge were filled with fun. Mr. Bobbsey had bought a barrel of apples, and when the family gathered about the fireplace they were put to roast in the heat of the glowing embers.

Corn was popped, and then it was eaten with salt and butter on top, or with melted sugar poured over it. Sometimes they would make candy, and once when they did this a funny thing happened.

Bert, Nan, Flossie, and Freddie, with the two cousins, had been out in the kitchen making a panful of the sweets. I must say that Dinah did the most work, but the children always declared that they made the candy. Anyhow, Dinah always washed the pans and dishes afterward.

"Now we'll set it out on the back steps to cool," said Nan, "and then we'll pull it into sticks."

The candy was soon in the condition for "pulling," and, putting butter on their fingers so the sweet stuff would not stick to them, the children began their fun.

The more they pulled the candy the harder it got and the lighter in color. Flossie and Freddie soon tired of the work that was hard on their little arms, and Nan set their rolls of candy outside again to cool, ready for eating.

All at once a great howling was heard at the back stoop, and Flossie cried, "Oh, someone is taking my candy!"

Bert laid the lump he was pulling down on the table, and rushed to the kitchen door. As he looked out he laughed.

"Oh, look!" he cried. "Snap tried to eat your candy, Freddie, and it's stuck to his jaws. He can't get his mouth open!"

This was just what had happened. Snap, playing around outside, had smelled the cooling candy. He was fond of sweets and in a moment had bitten on a big chunk. In an instant his jaws seemed glued together, and he set up a howl of pain and surprise.

"Oh, my lovely candy!" cried Freddie. "You bad Snap!"

"I guess Snap is punished enough," said Mrs. Bobbsey, coming to the kitchen to find out what the trouble was. And the poor dog was. He would not get his jaws open for some time, so sticky was the candy, and finally Bert had to put his pet's mouth in warm water, holding it there until the candy softened. Then Snap could open his jaws, and get rid of the rest of the sweet stuff in his mouth. He looked very much surprised at what had happened.

Freddie was given more candy to pull, and this time he set the pan in which he put it up high where no dog could get at it.

With the roasting of apples, making of popcorn, and pulling of candy, many pleasant evenings were spent. Then came a thaw, and some rain that carried off most of the snow. A freeze followed, and the lake was frozen over solidly.

"Now for skates and our ice boat!" cried Bert, and the fun started as soon as the lake was safe. The children had many good times, often going up to the nearest village in the ice boat.

Sometimes Bert had races with other ice boats, and occasionally he won even against larger craft that were bought from a store instead of being homemade. Almost as often the *Ice Bird* came in last. But Bert and the others did not care. They were having a good time.

Bert met Danny Rugg in the woods one day, and spoke to him about the snowslide. Danny said he had had nothing to do with it, but Bert did not believe the bully.

Then came a spell of fine warm weather, and as there was no snow on the ground, Bert, Nan, Dorothy, and Harry decided to take a long walk one afternoon. Nan wanted to get some views with her new camera.

So interested did they all become that they

never noticed how late it was, nor how far they had come.

"Oh, we must turn back!" cried Nan, when she did realize that it would soon be dark. "We're a good way from Snow Lodge."

"Oh, we can easily get back," declared Bert. "I know the path."

But though Bert might know the path they had come by daylight, it was quite different to find it after dark. However, he led the way, certain that he was going right. But when they had gone on for some distance, and saw no familiar landmarks, Nan stopped and asked: "Are you sure this is the right path, Bert? I don't remember passing any of these rocks," and she pointed to a group of them under some trees.

"I don't, either," said Dorothy.

"Well, maybe this path leads into the right one," suggested Harry. "Let's keep on a little further."

There seemed to be nothing else to do, so forward they went. Then a few flakes of snow began to fall, and they rapidly increased until the air was white with them. It made the scene a little lighter, but it caused Bert and the others to worry a good deal.

"I hope this isn't going to be much of a storm," said Bert in a low voice to Harry.

"Why not? It would make good sleigh-riding."

"Yes, but it's no fun to be in the woods when it storms, especially at night and when you're—lost."

"Lost!" cried Harry. "Are we lost?"

"I'm afraid so," Bert answered solemnly. "I haven't seen anything that looked like the path we came over for a long time. I guess we're lost all right."

"Oh! Oh!" cried Dorothy.

"Will we have to stay out in the woods all night?" Nan wanted to know.

Bert shook his head sadly.

"I'm afraid so," he said.

CHAPTER 17

HENRY BURDOCK

WITH the wind blowing about them, whirling the snowflakes into their faces, and with night fast coming on, the four young folks stood close together, looking at one another. Bert's solemn words had filled the hearts of the others with fear. Then Harry, sturdy country boy that he was, exclaimed, "Oh, don't let's give up so easily, Bert. Many a time I've been off in the woods and thought I was lost, when a little later I'd make a turn and be on the road home. Maybe we can do that now."

"Oh, I do hope so!" murmured Dorothy.

"Let's try!" exclaimed Nan, taking hold of her brother's arm.

"Wait a minute!" exclaimed Bert as Harry and Dorothy were about to start off. "Do you know where you're going?"

"We're going back that way," declared Harry, pointing off to the left.

"Why, that way?" asked Bert.

"I think that's the way to Snow Lodge," was the answer. "We've tried lots of other ways, and haven't struck the right one, so it can't do any harm to go a new way."

"Now just hold on," advised Bert. "I don't mean to say that I know more than you about it, Harry, but it does seem to me that it won't do any good to wander off that way, especially if you're not sure it's the right path. We'll only get more lost than we are, if that's possible."

"Well, maybe you're right," admitted Harry. "But we can't stay here all night, that's for sure."

"Of course not," added Dorothy, looking around with a shiver. The snow seemed to be coming down harder than ever and the cold wind blew with greater force.

"We may have to stay here," said Bert. "But don't let that scare you," he said quickly, as he saw Dorothy and his sister clutch at each other and turn pale. "We can build a sort of shelter that will keep us warm, and there won't be any danger of freezing."

"No, but how about starving?" asked Harry. "I'm real hungry now."

"We had a good dinner," observed Dorothy. "If we don't get anything more to eat until morning I guess we can stand it. But I do hope we can find some sort of shelter."

"We'll have to make one, I guess," said Nan, looking about her.

"That's right," cried Bert. "It's the only way. If we go wandering about looking for shelter we may get into trouble. We'll make one of our own. There's a good place over by that clump of trees. We can cut down some branches, stand them up around the trees, and make some sort of tent. Then, when the snow has covered it, we'll be real warm."

"Well, let's start building that snow tent," proposed Harry. "It will give us something to do, and moving about is warmer than standing still. I know that much anyhow."

"Yes, it is," agreed Bert. "Come on girls, Harry and I will cut the branches and you can stack them up."

Bert led the way to where three trees grew close together in a sort of triangle. The trees had low branches and it would be an easy matter to stand other branches up against them, one end on the ground, and so make a fairly good shelter.

With their pocketknives Bert and Harry began cutting branches from the evergreen trees that grew all about. As fast as they were cut the girls took them, and piled them up as best they could. All the while the wind blew the falling snow about, and it became darker.

"Oh, if we only had some sort of a fire!" exclaimed Nan.

"A fire?" said her brother.

"That's so," agreed Dorothy. "It would not be so lonesome then, and it would scare away—the bears!" and she looked over her shoulder in some fear.

"Bears!" cried Bert. "There aren't any within a hundred miles, unless they're tame ones. But we might as well have a fire. I never thought of that. I've got a box of matches. Harry, if you'll gather wood and make the fire, I'll keep on cutting branches. We've got almost enough, anyhow."

"Sure, I will!" said the other boy, and soon he had scraped away the snow from a spot on the ground, and had piled some sticks on it. He managed to find some dry twigs and leaves in a hollow stump, and these served to start a blaze. The wood was rather wet and it smoked a great deal, but soon some of the wood had caught and there was a cheerful fire reflecting redly on the white snow that was falling faster than ever.

"That's something like!" cried Bert, coming over to the blaze to warm his cold fingers. "We'll get a pile of wood and keep the fire going all night. Then, if any of our folks come looking for us, they can see it."

Harry, who had just come up with an armful of wood, plunged his hands into his pockets to warm them. The next moment he uttered a joyful cry, and drew out two small packages.

"Look!" he cried. "Here's our supper!"

"Supper?" asked Bert, slowly. "What do you mean?"

"It's chocolate candy," went on Harry. "I forgot I had it, but it's fine stuff when you're hungry. Lots of travelers use it when they can't get anything else to eat. Here, I'll divide it, and we'll imagine we're having a fine feast."

He was about to do this when Bert suddenly exclaimed, "Wait a minute! I have a better plan than that if I can only find a tin can. Everyone look for one. There may have been picnickers here during the summer, and they may have left a lot of tin cans."

"But what do you want of one?" asked Nan.

"I'll tell you if I find one," said her brother. "If I told you now, and we didn't pick up one, you'd be disappointed."

But they were not to be, for a little later Harry, kicking about in the snow, turned up a rusty tin can.

"That's it!" cried Bert. "Now we'll put some snow in it, and melt it over the fire. That will give us water, and when it boils we'll be sure the can is clean. Then we'll melt more snow and have hot chocolate. We'll dissolve the chocolate candy in the water, Harry, and drink it. That will be something hot for us, and better than if we ate the cold candy. I've got a folding drinking cup we can use."

"Say, that's a fine idea!" cried Dorothy. "Bert, you're wonderful."

"Oh, no, the idea just popped into my head," he replied.

The can, with some snow in it, was soon on the fire, and in a little while steam arising from it told that the water, formed from the melting snow, was boiling. They rinsed the can out carefully, made more hot water, and then put in the chocolate candy, saving half for another time.

Nan and Dorothy took turns stirring it with a clean stick until the mixture was foamy and hot. Then it was passed around in the single drinking cup.

"Oh, but I feel so much better now," sighed Nan, after taking her share. "So warm and comfortable!"

"So do I!" exclaimed Dorothy, and the boys admitted that the drink of chocolate was very good, even though it had no milk in it.

Then they finished making the shelter, brought up more wood for the night, and went in the little snow tent. Though it was only partly covered with a coating of white flakes, it was already warm and cozy and they knew that they were in no danger of freezing.

As much of the snow as possible was scraped away from the ground inside, and thick hemlock branches were laid down for a sort of carpet. Then, with the cheerful fire going outside, the four young people prepared to spend the night. That it would be lonesome they well knew, but they hoped Mr. Bobbsey would come and find them, perhaps with a searching party.

The warm chocolate, the warmth of the fire, the effect of the wind, weariness of the long walk, and the work of making a shelter, all combined to make the boys and girls sleepy in spite of their strange situation. First one and then the other would nod off, to awake with a start, until finally they were all asleep.

How long had he been slumbering thus in the little snow tent, Bert did not know. He suddenly awoke with a start, and listened. Yes, he heard something! The sound of someone tramping through the woods. A heavy body forcing its way through the bushes!

At first Bert's heart beat rapidly, and he thought of wild animals. Then he realized that none was near Snow Lodge. He glanced about. The campfire was burning only dimly and by the light of it, as it came in through the opening of the shelter, the boy could see the others sleeping, curled up on the soft branches.

The sound of someone approaching sounded louder. Bert looked about for some sort of weapon. There was none in the tent. Then he almost laughed at himself.

"How silly!" he exclaimed. "Of course it's father, or someone looking for us. I'll give a call."

He crawled to the edge of the shelter, looked out, and raised his voice in a shout: "Hello there! Here we are! Father, is that you?"

Those inside the little snow-covered tent awoke with a start. Bert tossed some light wood on the fire and it blazed up brightly. By its glow the boy saw, coming into the circle of light, a man dressed in thick, heavy garments, with a coonskin cap on his head. Over his shoulder was a gun, and he had some rabbits and birds slung at his back.

"Hello!" called the man to Bert, who was now outside the little tent. "Who are you?"

"Bert Bobbsey," was the answer. "My sister and cousins are here. We got lost and made this shelter. Were you looking for us?"

"Well, not exactly," said the hunter slowly, as he leaned on his gun, and looked at the fire. Then he looked at Bert and next at Nan, Dorothy, and Harry, who by this time had come from the tent.

"Not exactly, but maybe it's a good thing I found you. The storm is growing worse. What did you say your name was?"

"Bert Bobbsey."

The hunter started.

"Any relation to Mr. Richard Bobbsey?" he asked.

"He's my father."

"You don't say so! Well, I'm glad to hear that. It will give me a chance to do him a good turn. I'm Henry Burdock," the hunter went on.

It was the turn of Bert and Nan to be surprised.

"Henry Burdock!" repeated Bert. "Are you the nephew of Mr. Carford?"

"Yes," was the low reply. "Do you know him?"

"Why, we're stopping at his place–Snow Lodge," said Bert. "We got lost coming from there to take some pictures. Oh, Mr. Burdock, can you take us back there?"

"Snow Lodge–Snow Lodge," said the hunter slowly. His voice was sad, as though the place had bitter memories for him.

CHAPTER 18

SNOWBALLS

"ARE we very far from Snow Lodge?" asked Nan, after a pause. "We didn't think we would have any trouble getting back to it."

"You're about three miles away, and the path is hard to find in the darkness and storm," said the young hunter slowly. "Let me think what is best to do."

He remained leaning on his gun, staring into the fire, which was now burning brightly. Then he spoke again.

"You youngsters certainly have made this a fine shelter. I couldn't have done it much better myself. It's just the thing to keep out the cold wind."

"We thought we'd have to stay here all night," said Bert. "We made some hot chocolate. We've got a little left. Will you take some?"

"No, thank you," replied Henry Burdock. "I generally carry a little to eat with me, and I just finished my night lunch. I had some cold coffee that I warmed up, too. I'm sorry, but if I had known I was going to meet you folks I'd have saved some."

"Oh, we're all right," declared Harry. "We can finish our chocolate, and then perhaps you can show us the way back to Snow Lodge."

"Yes," spoke Henry Burdock slowly, "I could do that. I know the way well enough. But it's a hard path to travel in the storm, and after dark. I don't believe you girls could manage it," and he looked at Nan and Dorothy.

"Oh, yes, we could!" Nan exclaimed. "We've had a good rest, and papa and mamma will be so anxious about us!"

"I'd like first-rate to take you all home," said the hunter, "but I think I have a better plan. My shack isn't far from here. I could take you all there, and you could stay until morning. Then I could go to Snow Lodge and tell them you were all right. When it was daylight they could come for you in the sled."

"Maybe that would be best," agreed Bert.

"But won't it be too much of a trip for you?" asked Nan.

"No, I'm used to roaming about the woods," said Mr. Carford's nephew, with a sad smile. "A few miles more or less won't make any difference, and I know every inch of this forest. I've had to," he added. "It's the only home I have now."

"Yes, we—we heard about you," said Nan quickly, and there was kindness in her voice. "It's too bad your uncle acted as he did, and sent you away."

"Well, he thought he was doing right," said Henry. "I don't know as I blame him. Your father, though, he stuck to me, and I'm glad I can do his children a favor."

"Indeed, it seems too much to ask," spoke Dorothy, for Nan had whispered to her and Harry the details of the story of the missing money that Henry Burdock was suspected of taking.

"I don't mind," said the hunter. "I didn't do much walking today. Game was not very plentiful, though I got some. Now I'll lead you to my shack. It's small, but it's warm, and you can be comfortable there until daylight. I was walking through the woods when I saw the flicker of your fire, and came up to see what it was."

"And I couldn't imagine what it was I heard when I woke up," said Bert. "I was a bit frightened at first," he admitted, with a smile.

"I don't blame you," said Henry. "And, since we are talking about Snow Lodge, I want to say that I never took that money. It was on the mantel in the living room, just as my uncle says it was, for I saw it. I don't deny that I would have been glad to have it, for I had been foolish and I owed more than I could pay. But I never took that roll of bills."

"Have you any idea who did?" asked Bert.

"Not in the least. And as I was the only one in the house, besides my uncle, of course it made it look as if I had taken it, especially as the money totally disappeared. But I never laid a hand on it."

"It is too bad," said Bert. "Maybe some day the bills will be found and you will be cleared."

"I hope so," sighed Henry. "But it's been some years now, and my uncle has considered me a thief all that while. I've gotten so I don't much care anymore. Living in the woods makes you sort of that way. You do a lot of thinking.

"But there!" exclaimed the young hunter, straightening up. "This isn't doing you children any good. I'd better be taking you to my place instead of staying here. Have you anything to carry?"

"My camera—that's all," said Nan. "I'll get it," and she darted into the shelter after it. Then, when the fire had been extinguished so there would be no danger of it spreading, the young folks set off after Henry Burdock, who led the way. He seemed to know it, even in the darkness, but of course the white snow on the ground made the path rather easy to pick out.

In a short time they came to a log cabin, which was the "shack" the hunter had mentioned. It was the work of but a few minutes to open it and blow into flames the fire that was smoldering on the hearth. A lamp had been lighted and the place was warm and cozy enough for anyone.

"Oh, this is fine!" cried Nan. "If the folks knew we were here they'd know we were all right and not worry."

"They'll soon know it," said Mr. Burdock. "I'm going to set off at once for Snow Lodge. Will you be afraid to stay here?"

"Not a bit of it!" exclaimed Bert, and the others agreed with him.

Leaving the game he had shot, Henry Burdock started off again through the storm-swept woods while Bert and the others made themselves at home in the cabin. Mr. Burdock had showed them where he kept his food, and the boys and girls enjoyed a midnight lunch, for it was now after twelve o'clock.

It was about three in the morning when the hunter came back and found his young friends asleep. He let himself in quietly, and not until daylight, when they awoke, did he tell them of his trip.

He had reached Snow Lodge safely, where he found Mr. and Mrs. Bobbsey distraught over the absence of the children. Mr. Bobbsey and Sam had searched as well as they could, and they were just going off to arouse some nearby farmers and make a more thorough hunt when Mr. Burdock came in.

That his news was welcome need not be said,

and Mrs. Bobbsey wept for joy when she knew that her children and the others were safe. They wanted the young hunter to remain until daylight, and go back with them in the sled, but he said he would rather go on to his cabin now. Perhaps he did not feel that he should remain in Snow Lodge, from where his uncle had driven him in anger years before.

Mr. Burdock gave Mr. Bobbsey directions how to find the cabin and, as soon as the first streak of daylight showed, the lumber merchant and Sam set off in the big sled. Flossie and Freddie were not awake, or they might have been taken along.

And a little later Bert, Nan, Dorothy, and Harry were safe in Snow Lodge once more.

For some days after this the weather was stormy, so the young folks could not go far from Snow Lodge. But they managed to have good times indoors, or out in the big barn.

Then came another thaw, and a freeze followed some days later, making good skating. One afternoon Bert proposed to Harry that they go for a trip on the ice boat.

"But not too far," cautioned his father. "We don't want you to get lost again."

"No, we'll only go a mile or so," said Bert. "Want to come, Nan and Dorothy?"

The girls did, and so also did Flossie and

Freddie, but their mother would not allow this. So Freddie got out his engine and played fireman, while his little sister put her walking and talking doll through her performance. Snap the trick dog, with many barks, raced off with Bert and the older children.

The *Ice Bird* sailed well that day, skimming over the frozen lake at a fast pace, and the children greatly enjoyed the sport. Snap sat on the boat with the others, looking as though he liked it as well as anyone.

They sailed up the lake for some distance and then got out to look for a cave that Bert had heard was a short distance from shore. They did not find it at once, but while they were climbing up a little hill, thinking the cave might be somewhere near it, Harry was suddenly startled to receive a snowball on his ear.

"Ouch!" he cried. "Who threw that?"

They all stopped and looked around. No one was in sight.

"Maybe it fell off a tree," suggested Nan.

"It came too hard for that," declared Harry. "It was thrown."

They looked about again but, seeing no one, went on. Then, suddenly there came another ball, and Dorothy cried: "There, that came out of a tree, for I saw it. Right over there," and she pointed.

"Then if it came out of a tree someone is up the tree!" declared Bert. "And I'm going to see who it is."

As he rushed forward a snowball struck him full in the face.

CHAPTER 19

SNAP IS GONE

DOROTHY screamed, and turned back toward Nan when she saw Bert struck with the snowball. But plucky Nan kept on.

"That must be Danny Rugg!" cried Bert's sister. "No one else around here would be as mean as that!"

Bert stopped a moment to brush the snow from his eyes, and then he rushed toward the tree.

"Who is it?" cried Harry.

"I don't know—but I'm going to find out," was Bert's answer. "Come along!"

The two boys hurried on, the girls lingering in the rear.

Again a snowball flew out of the tree, but it struck no one, though coming nearer to Nan.

By this time Bert was close to the tree. It was a hemlock, and the branches were quite thick, but Bert got a glimpse of someone hiding among them.

"Come down out of that!" Bert cried. "I see you!"

There was no answer.

"What do you mean by hitting us?" asked Harry angrily. "We didn't do anything to you."

Still there was no answer.

"I'm going to do some snowballing on my own account," spoke Bert. "Here goes!"

He quickly made a hard ball and, circling around the tree to find an opening in the branches, he saw the figure of the boy more plainly.

"Danny Rugg!" cried Bert. "So it's you, is it? First you start a snowslide down on us and then you snowball us. This has got to stop. Take that!"

Bert threw, but though his aim was good, Danny (for it really was the bully) managed to climb up higher in the tree, and the snowball broke into pieces against the branches.

"Ha, ha!" laughed Danny.

"Oh, there's plenty more snow," said Harry, "and you can't have an awful lot up there."

His answer was another snowball, which struck him on the shoulder, doing no harm. Danny must have taken some snow ammunition up the tree with him and, in addition, there was a supply of the white flakes on the wide branches of the hemlock.

Bert and Harry both began throwing snowballs up into the tree, but they were at a disadvantage for their missiles broke to pieces against the trunk or branches. On the other hand Danny could wait his chances and hit them when they came within sight.

"This won't do!" exclaimed Bert after a bit. "We've got to get him out of that tree."

"How can we?" asked Harry. "Climb up it, and pull him down?"

"Oh, don't do that!" cried Nan. "You might get hurt."

"Yes, that would be risky," admitted Bert. "One of us might slip and fall. Hey you, Danny Rugg!" cried Bert. "Come on down, and we'll give you a fair show. Only one of us will tackle you at a time."

"Huh! Think I'm coming down?" asked Danny. "I'm not afraid of you, but I'm going to stay up here."

"Oh, are you?" asked Bert, as he thought of a new plan. "We'll see about that. Come here, Harry."

From the tree Danny looked down anxiously while Harry and Bert whispered together. The girls had walked off to one side.

"How are you going to get him down?" asked Harry.

"Cut the tree," answered Bert. "It's only a small one."

"But we can't even cut that down with our knives."

"I know. But on the ice boat is that hatchet father gave me to take to be sharpened. I forgot about it on the way up the lake, and I was going to do it on the way back. There's a blacksmith shop in the big cove. But the hatchet is sharp enough to chop down this tree. We'll get it and give Danny a good scare."

"That's what we will. You stay here and I'll run down and get it."

Harry started off on a run, and Danny, still up the tree, wondered what plan was afoot. The bully had been out for a walk when he saw Bert and the others coming up the hill. He quickly climbed the tree in order to throw snowballs at them.

When Harry came back with the hatchet Bert once more called to Danny.

"Are you coming down to fight fair? I give you my promise that only one of us will tackle you at a time. You can have your choice."

"I'm not coming down!" cried Danny.

"Chop away, Harry!" called Bert. "I guess I can pepper him with a few snowballs if he tries to throw any at you."

The tree trunk was not very thick, and the hatchet was fairly sharp. In a little while the tree began swaying.

"I say now, stop that!" cried Danny, trying to get a better hold in the branches.

"Better come down before you fall," suggested Bert, who had a pile of snowballs ready.

The tree swayed more and more. Bert and

Harry knew that even if Danny fell with it he could not get hurt in the soft drifts. So Harry kept on chopping.

The tree swayed more and more. There was a cracking sound. Then Danny cried, "Don't chop anymore—I'm coming down!"

"Get ready, Harry!" called Bert. "We'll give him some of the same kind of a thing he gave us!"

In another instant Danny jumped, and as the swaying tree sprang back when relieved of his weight, Bert and Harry leaped forward to pelt the bully with snowballs.

Danny tried to fight back, but he was no match for the two of them, and soon he began to look like a snow image, so well was he plastered with white flakes.

"Give it to him!" cried Bert, whose face still stung where Danny had struck him with a snowball.

"That's what I will," agreed Harry, whose ear was quite sore.

For a time Danny said nothing, but tried to block off the rain of snowballs, and threw back some of his own. Then, as he was almost overwhelmed by the ones Harry and Bert threw, the bully cried, "Stop! Stop! I've had enough! I won't bother you anymore!"

Danny was soon out of sight, running off in the

direction of his father's lumber tract, and soon Bert and the others went back to the ice boat.

They stopped at the blacksmith shop to leave the hatchet, and reached home after a little sail on the *Ice Bird.*

"Did anything happen this time?" asked Freddie, as he greeted them on the return to Snow Lodge.

"Not much," replied Bert. "We just had a snow fight, that's all."

The skating and ice-boating lasted for some time, and the girls and boys had lots of fun. Nights were spent in popping corn, telling stories, roasting apples, and once, in the big sled, they all went to an entertainment in a nearby school hall.

It was on returning from this that Dinah met them at the door asking, "Did you all take Snap with you?"

"Take Snap? No," said Mr. Bobbsey.

The children began to look alarmed.

"He was here," said Dinah. "But I can't find him now. He's missing."

CHAPTER 20

THE BIG STORM

FOR a moment they all looked at one another by turns. Flossie and Freddie showed the most alarm. Bert started for the outside door, as though intending to make a search for his pet. Mr. Bobbsey questioned Dinah.

"Are you sure," he asked, "that Snap isn't around?"

"I'm sure," she replied. "I called him to come have something to eat, but he wasn't around."

"I wonder if he could have followed after us, and got lost," said Mrs. Bobbsey. "Did any of you see him trailing us?"

"He did come a little way when we started off," came from Dorothy.

"Yes, but Dinah called him back, didn't you?" asked Nan of the cook.

"Yes, that's what I did. And Snap came. Then, to make sure he wouldn't sneak off and follow you again, I shut him up in the kitchen and gave him a chicken bone. After a while I let him out. He ran around, kind of disappointed-like, and came back. Then I didn't look for him until a little while ago, but he was gone."

"We'll take a look around," Mr. Bobbsey said, and with Bert and Harry he went outside. But neither calling nor whistling brought any bark from Snap. Nor did he come bounding joyfully up, as he usually did when summoned. The darkness about Snow Lodge was quiet. There was no sign of Snap.

"He's gone off in the woods and is lost," said Harry.

"Snap knows better than to get lost," declared Bert. "He could find his way home from almost anywhere. I think he must have followed someone away."

"Would he do that?" asked Harry.

"He might with someone he knew if that person petted him," said Mr. Bobbsey.

"That hunter—Henry Burdock!" suddenly exclaimed Bert. "Snap made great friends with him when he met him out in the woods the other day, and Henry said he'd make a fine hunting dog."

"I don't believe Henry Burdock would entice our dog away," said Mr. Bobbsey with a shake of his head.

"Oh, of course I don't mean on purpose," said

Bert. "But Snap may have been running about in the woods at dusk when he met Henry. Then he may have followed him, for Snap is part hunting dog and he gets crazy when he sees a gun. Maybe he followed Henry, and wouldn't be driven back through the snow."

"Maybe that's so," agreed Mr. Bobbsey. "In that case Snap will be all right, and we can get him in the morning. So don't worry anymore."

They went back in the Lodge to find Freddie and Flossie almost in tears. But the little twins felt better when it was explained to them that Snap might after all be safe with the young hunter.

"And will you get him first thing in the morning?" asked Freddie.

The following day was so nice that Flossie and Freddie were allowed to go with Bert, Nan, Harry, and Dorothy to the cabin of Henry Burdock to look for Snap. The small twins were put on two sleds, the older children taking turns pulling them.

They easily found Henry's cabin, having been there several times since the night they spent in it. The hunter was just about to start off on a trip.

"Where's Snap?" called Bert eagerly.

"Snap? I haven't seen him since that day I met you with him in the woods," answered the hunter.

"What! Isn't he here?" asked Harry.

Then they told of the missing dog. But Henry Burdock had not seen him.

"Where can he be?" spoke Nan wonderingly.

Flossie and Freddie began to cry.

"Oh, a bear has Snap!" wailed Flossie.

"No, he hasn't!" declared Bert. "We'll find him."

"But where can he be?" said Dorothy. "Is there anyone else around here who might take him?"

Bert and Nan thought of the same thing at the same time.

"Danny Rugg," they exclaimed.

"What do you mean?" asked Henry Burdock.

"He's a mean boy who is camping with his father near us," explained Bert. "Harry and I pelted him good with snowballs the other day, after he bothered us. I think he has enticed Snap away."

"Would your dog go with him?"

"Yes, he's friendly with Danny, for sometimes Danny is fairly good and comes to our house. If he offered Snap a nice bone he might go with Danny."

"Then I advise you to have a look over where Danny is camping," said the young hunter.

It was quite a trip back to Snow Lodge and then over to the Rugg lumber camp, and Mrs. Bobbsey thought it too far to take Flossie and Freddie, so they were left behind on the second trip, Nan and Dorothy going with Bert and Harry.

They saw Danny Rugg standing in front of a log cabin that was on the edge of a lumber camp. The bully seemed uneasy at the sight of Harry and Bert and called out, "If you're coming here to make any trouble I'll tell my father on you. He's right over there."

"We're not going to make any trouble, Danny Rugg, if you don't," said Bert slowly. "But we came for Snap, our dog."

"I don't know anything about your dog," answered Danny in surly tones.

"I think you do," said Bert quietly. Then raising his voice he called, "Snap! Snap! Where are you, old fellow? Snap!"

There was a moment of silence and then, from a small cabin some distance away, came loud barks.

"There's Snap! That's our dog!" cried Nan joyfully, and at the sound of her voice the barking grew louder. There could also be heard the rattling of a chain.

"You've got him tied, Danny Rugg!" cried Bert, angrily. "Let him go at once or I'll hit you!"

"Don't you dare touch me!" cried the bully. "And you get off our land!"

"Not until I get my dog," said Bert firmly.

He started for the cabin where the dog was, but Danny stepped in front of him. Bert shoved Danny to one side, and just then Mr. Rugg came up.

"Here! What does this mean?" he asked. "Bert Bobbsey, you here?"

"Yes, sir. I came after my dog. Danny has him tied up!"

"Danny, is this so?" asked Mr. Rugg, who knew some of his son's mean ways and had tried in vain to break him of them. "Have you Bert's dog?"

"Well, maybe it is his dog. It was dark when he followed me home last night, and I tied him in that shack."

"I guess he wouldn't have followed you if you hadn't coaxed him," said Bert.

"Well, I couldn't drive him back," went on Danny, but the Bobbseys believed that he had deliberately coaxed Snap off to make trouble.

"Let the dog out at once," said Mr. Rugg to his son, and Danny had to do so, though he was angry and sullen over it.

How Snap leaped about his master and mistress and their cousins! How delightfully he barked! And his tail wagged to and fro so fast that it looked like two tails, as Freddie said afterward.

"Poor Snap!" said Bert, as he patted his pet. "And so you were tied up all night? It was a mean trick!" and his eyes flashed on Danny, who looked on sneeringly.

"I am sorry for this, Bert," said Mr. Rugg. "If I

had known Danny enticed away your dog I would have made him bring it back. Now I am going to punish him. You go back home today, Danny. You can't stay in the lumber camp any longer."

Danny felt bad, of course, but it served him right.

The Bobbseys and their cousins lost no time in getting back to Snow Lodge with Snap, who was hugged so much by Flossie and Freddie that Dinah said, "That dog must be almost starved. Let him have some breakfast, and then hug him!"

"Oh, but we like him so!" cried Flossie.

So Snap was restored, and Danny was sent home out of the woods, so there was no more trouble from him.

In the days that followed, the Bobbsey twins at Snow Lodge had many more good times. They made snow forts and had snow battles, they made big snowmen and threw snowballs at them, and went on sleigh rides or skated and ice-boated, and played around generally to their hearts' content.

Occasionally the two older boys went on long tramps with Henry Burdock as he visited his traps. They invited him to come to Snow Lodge, but he said, "No, I'm not coming there until I can prove to my uncle that I never touched his money. Then I'll come."

One day, when Bert and Harry had been in the

woods with the young hunter, he said to them, "Don't go far away from Snow Lodge tomorrow, boys."

"Why not?" asked Bert.

"Because I think we're in for a big storm, and you might easily get lost again. Unless I'm mistaken, it's going to snow hard before morning."

Henry Burdock proved a true weather prophet, for when the Bobbseys and the others got up the next morning the ground was covered with a mantle of newly fallen snow and more was sifting down from the clouds. The wind, too, was blowing fiercely.

"It's going to be a bad storm," said Mr. Bobbsey, looking out after breakfast. "Luckily we have plenty of wood and plenty to eat."

The wind howled around Snow Lodge while the white flakes came down thicker and faster.

"Maybe we'll be snowed in," said Nan.

"That would be fun!" cried Bert.

CHAPTER 21

THE FALLING TREE

HOW the wind did blow! How the snow swirled and drifted around the old farmhouse! But within, all were warm and comfortable. The fire on the open hearth was kept roaring up the chimney, Sam piling on log after log. In the cozy kitchen Dinah kept at her work over the range, singing old plantation melodies.

The blowing wind and the drifting snow kept up all day. Flossie and Freddie begged to be allowed to go out for a little while, but their mother would not think of it. Bert and Harry tried to go a little way beyond the barn, but were driven back by the cold, wintry blasts. Dorothy and Nan managed to have a good time in the attic of the old house, dressing up in some clothes of a bygone era, which they found in some trunks.

"My! I hope the chimneys don't blow off!" exclaimed Mrs. Bobbsey, as a particularly fierce blast shook the old house. "A fire now would be dreadful."

"I don't imagine there is much danger," said Mr. Bobbsey with a laugh. "The way they built houses and chimneys when Snow Lodge was put up was different from nowadays. They were built to stay."

"Oh, but this is a terrible storm!"

"Yes, and it seems to be getting worse," agreed Mr. Bobbsey. "I hope no one is out in it. But, as I said, we have plenty to eat, and wood to keep us warm, and that is all we can ask."

The day slowly passed, but toward afternoon Flossie and Freddie grew fretful from having been kept in. They were used to going out of doors in almost any kind of weather.

"Come on up in the attic with us," suggested Nan, "and we'll have a sort of circus."

"And Snap can do tricks," cried Freddie, "and I'll give an exhibition with my fire engine."

"Of course!" exclaimed Dorothy, and the little Bobbsey twins forgot their fretfulness in a new series of games.

Harder blew the wind, and fiercer fell the snow. The path Mr. Bobbsey had shoveled was soon filled up again. Out at the back door was a drift that covered the rear stoop.

"If this keeps up we will be snowed in," said Mr. Bobbsey to his wife as they prepared to lock up for the night.

They were gathered around the big open fire, popping corn and roasting apples, when a louder blast of wind than ever shook the house.

"Oh, what a night!" said Mrs. Bobbsey, with a shudder. "I wish we were in our home again!"

Hardly had she spoken when there came a fearful crash, and the whole house trembled. At the same time a blast of cold wind swept through it, scattering the fire on the hearth.

"Oh, what was that?" cried Mrs. Bobbsey.

"That old apple tree, at the corner of the house," said Mr. Bobbsey. "The storm has blown it over, and it has smashed a corner of the Lodge. Don't be afraid. We'll be all right," and he ran to close the door to keep out the cold wind.

CHAPTER 22

THE MISSING MONEY

"WHAT happened?" asked Mrs. Bobbsey, when her husband had come back after going out to take a look around. "Is the house safe?"

"As safe as ever," he answered. "Just as I told you, the old apple tree blew over and smashed the corner of the house near this living room. That's why we felt the crash so. But there is no great harm done. We can keep this door closed and not use that other part of the house at all. We have room enough without it. The wind and storm can't get at us here."

"I sure thought the house was coming down," said Dinah, who had run in from the kitchen at the sound of the crash.

"It was a hard blow," said Bert. "Look, all the ashes are scattered," and he pointed to where the wind had blown them about the hearth.

Dinah soon swept them up, however, and more wood was put on the fire, and the Bobbseys were as comfortable as before. The part of the house which had been smashed by the tree was closed off from the rest.

Soon it was time to go to bed, but all night long the storm raged, making Snow Lodge tremble in the blast. Everyone was up early in the morning to see by daylight what damage had been done.

The sun rose clear, for the storm had passed. But oh what a lot of snow there was! In big drifts it was scattered all over the place, and one side door was snowed in completely and could not be opened. Sam had to shovel a lot of snow away from the kitchen steps before Dinah could go out.

"Let's go see where the tree fell," suggested Bert to Harry, when they were dressed. Nan and Dorothy joined them. They went to the corner of the house and there saw a strange sight. The old apple tree lay partly in the room into which it had crashed through the side of the house. And much snow had blown in also.

This room, however, was little used, except for storage, and there was nothing in it to be damaged save some old furniture. Bert and Harry made their way into the apartment, and the girls followed.

They were looking about at the odd sight when something in the corner of the room, along the wall that was next to the living room where the Bobbseys had spent the evening, caught Bert's eyes. He went toward it. He picked up a roll of what seemed to be green paper. It had been in a crack of the wall that had been made wider by the falling tree.

"Oh, look!" he cried. "What is this? Why, it's money!"

"A roll of bills!" added Harry, looking over his cousin's shoulder.

Slowly Bert unrolled them. There seemed to be considerable money there. One bill was a hundred-dollar one.

"Where did it come from?" asked Nan.

"From a crack in the wall," spoke her brother. "It must have slipped down, and the falling tree made the crack wider so I could see it."

"I wonder who could have put it there?" said Dorothy.

Bert and Nan looked at each other. The same thought came into their minds.

"The missing money!" cried Bert. "The roll of bills that Mr. Carford thought his nephew took! Can this be it?"

"Oh, if it only is!" murmured Nan. "Let's tell Papa right away!"

Carrying the money so strangely found, the young folks went into the house where Mr. and Mrs. Bobbsey were. The roll of bills was shown, and Mr. Bobbsey was much surprised.

"Do you think this can be the money Mr. Carford lost?" asked Bert.

"I shouldn't be surprised," said Mr. Bobbsey. "I'll take a look. Mr. Carford said he left it on the mantel in the living room. And you found it in the room back of that. I'll look."

Quickly he examined the mantel. Then he exclaimed, "Yes, that's how it happened. There is a crack up here, and the money must have slipped down into it. All these years it has been in between the walls until the falling tree made a break and showed where it was. Mr. Carford was mistaken. His nephew did not take the money. I always said so. It fell into the crack and remained hidden until the storm showed where it was."

"Oh, how glad I am!" cried Mrs. Bobbsey. "Now Henry's name can be cleared! Oh, if he were only here to know the good news!"

There seemed to be no doubt of it. Years before Mr. Carford had placed the money on the shelf of the living room. He probably did not know of the crack into which it slipped. The roll of bills had gone down between the walls, and only the breaking of them when the tree fell on the house brought the money to light.

"It is a strange thing," said Mr. Bobbsey. "The missing money is found after all these years, and in such a queer way! We must tell Henry as soon as possible, and Mr. Carford also."

Suddenly there came a knock on the door. Bert went to it and gave a cry of surprise. There stood the young hunter—Henry Burdock.

"I came over to see if you were all right," he said. "We have had a fearful storm. Part of my cabin was blown away, and I wondered how you fared at Snow Lodge. Are you all right?"

"Yes, Henry, we are," said Mr. Bobbsey. "And the storm was a good thing for you."

"I don't see how. My cabin is spoiled. I'll have to build it over again."

"You won't have to, Henry. You can come to live at Snow Lodge now."

"Never. Not until my name is cleared. I will never live at Snow Lodge until the missing money is found, and my uncle says I did not take it."

"Then you can come now, Henry," cried Mr. Bobbsey, holding out the roll of bills. "For the money is found and we can clear your name!"

"Is it possible!" exclaimed the young hunter in great and joyful surprise. "Oh, how I have prayed for this! The money found! Where was it? How did you find it?"

Then the story was told, the children having their share in it.

"I can't tell you how thankful I am," said the young hunter. "This means a lot to me. Now my uncle will know I am not a thief. I must go and tell him at once."

"No, I'll go," said Mr. Bobbsey. "I want to prove to him that I was right, after all, in saying you were innocent. You stay here until I bring him."

Mr. Bobbsey went off in the big sled with Sam to drive the horses. It was a hard trip on account of the drifts, but finally Newton was reached and Mr. Carford found. At first he could hardly believe that the money was found, but when he saw and counted it, finding it exactly the same as when he had put it on the shelf years before, he knew that he had done wrong in accusing Henry.

"And I'll tell him so, too," he said. "I'll beg his pardon, and he and I will live together again. Oh, how happy I am! Now I can go to Snow Lodge with a light heart."

Uncle and nephew met and clasped hands while tears stood in their eyes. After years of suffering they were friends again. It was a happy, loving time for all.

"And I'll never be so hasty again," said Mr. Carford. "Oh, what a happy day this is, after the big storm! We must have a big celebration. I know what I'll do. I'll get up a party and invite all the people in this part of the country. They all know that I accused Henry of taking that money. Now they must know that he did not. I will admit my mistake.

And that is what Mr. Carford did. He sent out many invitations to an old-fashioned party at Snow Lodge. The place where the tree had crashed through and exposed the missing money was boarded up, and the house made cozy again.

Then came the party, and the Bobbseys were the guests of honor—particularly the twins and their cousins, for it was due to them, in a great measure, that the money had been found.

Mr. Carford stood up before everyone else and admitted how wrong he had been in saying his nephew had taken the money.

"But all our troubles are ended now," he said, "and Henry and I will live in Snow Lodge together. And we will always be glad to see you here—all of you—and most especially, the Bobbseys."

"Three cheers for the Bobbsey twins!" someone called.

The children were pleased at this praise. They did not know that soon they would be helping some other people. You may read about this in *The Bobbsey Twins on a Houseboat.*

Then followed a fine feast—a happy time for all, while Henry and his uncle received the good wishes of their friends and neighbors.

Snap raced around, barking and wagging his tail. Bert, Nan, Dorothy, Harry, and Flossie were here, there, everywhere, telling how the tree had blown down, and how they had found the money.

"Dear old Snow Lodge!" said Nan, when the party was over and the guests gone. "We will have to leave it soon! But perhaps we can come back some time."

"I'd like to," agreed Bert. "Next winter I am going to build a bigger ice boat, and sail all over the lake."

"And we'll make regular snowshoes, and go hunting in the woods," said Harry.

"But it will be summer before it is winter again," said Freddie. "I'm going to have a motor-boat and ride in it. And I'll take my fire engine along, and pump water."

"Can I come, with my doll?" asked Flossie.

"Yes, you may all come!" exclaimed Mamma Bobbsey, as she hugged the two little twins.

"And don't forget," said Mr. Carford, "that Snow Lodge is open in the summer as well as in the winter. I expect you Bobbsey twins to visit me once in a while. I never can thank you enough for finding that missing money."

"Neither can I," said Henry.

And now that the story is all told, we will say good-bye to the Bobbsey Twins and their friends.

The End